MOUNTAIN DEEP

BOOK IV OF THE ALISTAIR SAGA

J.M. KÆ

MOUNTAIN DEEP

By J.M. KÆ
© Copyright Information
Year of Publication 2024
United States of America
First Edition
All Rights Reserved
Paperback ISBN: 979-8321749074
Hardcover ISBN: 979-8321749487

Disclaimer: Persons, places, incidents, and actions written in this book and the Alistair Saga story are a work of fiction. Any resemblance to real persons, places, incidents, or actions written for the purpose of the story is coincidental.

All comments or questions can be addressed to:
www.joannakurczakwriting.com

It Matters Not How Deep The Pain Reaches,
The Fated One's Love Holds The Power To Heal The
Deepest Of Despairs

≈ Chapter 1 ≈

Zakopane. The serene self-proclaimed winter capital of Poland. Stretching from its high mountain peaks ruling over the beautifully picturesque highlands down to the valleys and gorges hiding mysteries not yet discovered. This land called out to Perseus Alistair. It called out to his reticent heart and introverted soul. He chose this region of Poland for a reason. He did so not out of necessity for solitude, but because he decided long ago that the life of a loner suited him. Why? He liked it - nay, he preferred it that way. Because his parents offered him a perfect example of two people who fell in love so deeply that they chose to defend their love over their lives.

He could not fathom yielding such power to someone else. The way he saw it, doing so would mean surrendering his basic need. A need for control. Control he could not foresee losing one quiet snowy morning, in the most unfathomable Twist-Of-Fate sort of way...

The day his life changed forever began as it usually did on a cold and wintery December day. December 24th to be exact. The snow, falling gently the night before, seized its soft gale to the first rays of the rising sun. Perseus loved that part of the day. The quietly simmering energy. The promise of a day not yet lived. The hours soon to come, full of possibilities. There was something to be said about the way the early morning rays of the sun caressed the crisp undisturbed snow. Perseus may have lived near the Ku Dziurze Gorge, beside the mountain stream bearing the same name, in a narrow valley leading up to the Gorge, but he loved the freedom the open mountain ranges offered him.

Was he an assassin? When the occasion called for it. Did he prefer to work alone? Very much so. His siblings referred to him as an unreformed mountain man, and the designation fit him to a 'T'. The only person whose existence he tolerated daily was the man who once saved his life. The man he thought of as his grandfather if he ever had one...

"Morning." A raspy voice greeted Perseus while he stood by the kitchen window and watched the snow glistening in the morning sun rays along the banks of the narrow and rocky 'Ku Dziurze' stream flowing down the mountain near his hidden mountain cottage.

"Morning, Alan," Perseus replied, with his back turned toward the man. He raised his espresso cup filled with the jet-black liquid, as if he were saluting the man who had just walked in from the cold.

"It is a fine dawn to begin a much-deserved vacation, don't You think?" The voice appeared to soften as the man approached Perseus, though he paused by the antique clay stove when he saw the packed backpack beside the stove. "I see You've already packed for the journey. Good. I presume it should not take more than a couple of days to reach Isola Bella, even with the holiday traffic."

"My means of travel differ somewhat from the usual mode of transportation," Perseus smirked into his cup and turned toward the man. "And I would hardly call visiting Caelum a vacation."

"Oh?" The man raised his eyebrow, and a hint of wit in his short retort could not have gone unnoticed. Not to Perseus.

"The Alistairs are a sizable bunch. But You must agree adding two more Alistairs into this world is quite admirable. Especially at once."

"I'll say." The man clicked his tongue. "To think falling in love would turn Caelum Alistair into a father material. And so soon."

"I saw it in his eyes when he saved Anya. Caelum has a big heart, even if he hides it well. It just surprised me he's welcoming twins on his first try," Perseus smirked in a purely Alistair cocky manner.

"He definitely gave J.J. Monroe and Rigel a run for their money. No wonder J.J. spared no time ensuring Aurora and little Seven will have a sibling so soon. Rigel better step up his game."

"Definitely. He already grew tired of Tom's teasing," Perseus shook his head. "Then again, with three Alistairs down, it's good that they put their minds to it. Better them not me."

"Even the most stubborn loners fall eventually," Alan retorted as he poured more water into the kettle.

"Are You speaking about me? Or about You?"

"Both. Years lived offer something to a man You youngsters seldom strive for."

"Experience?" Perseus smiled with confidence.

"Wisdom, dear Perseus."

"That is true," Perseus noted. "That's why I prefer these walls, these mountains, and these snow-covered hills. Odd how tables of humanity have turned. Society today acts more savage than the wilderness itself."

"I'd be careful about the way You speak. I would not call it wilderness. Nature might turn the tables on You," Alan pointed at him with a teaspoon before piling up a hefty amount of freshly ground coffee onto it.

"Wisdom? Or experience?" Perseus smirked with amusement at both the gesture and the man's words.

"Both." Alan smirked. "She might even play one on Your heart for referring to her as wilderness."

"I'm well aware of my secluded cabin and the secrets it hides. No woman will come here, I assure You." Perseus flashed his grin in return. "And I have faith in You watching my back to ensure it stays that way."

"As You wish," Alan shook his head and poured steaming water into his cup.

The men enjoyed a quiet breakfast worthy of mountain men. Perseus was about to rise from the kitchen table when his emergency phone rang. Both men looked at the phone in silence, exchanged looks, and knew what it meant.

"Don't tell me You're going to take that on Your day off?" Alan asked with hesitation.

"Tatra Volunteer Search and Rescue doesn't get days off," Perseus rose from the table, and went to answer the phone.

"Don't they know You're leaving?" Alan asked, gathering the plates and cups.

"I haven't left yet." Perseus moved his shoulders and picked up the phone. He stood still, listened to the dispatcher's information and instructions. "Understood. I'm on my way. I'll head there from here. I'll get there faster."

"How many?" Was all Alan asked.

"Four. A mother and her three sons. They never returned to their hotel last night."

"Last night...?" Alan set the plates down, worried. "In this weather? That doesn't amount to anything good."

"Exactly," Perseus agreed and walked out of the kitchen only to return in full rescue gear.

"Watch Yourself out there."

"I always do. I guess Caelum will have to wait a little longer for me."

"Oh? Look how that worked out for You?" The man grinned, but the grin disappeared. "You may not like kids too much, but I hope those You're leaving to find are found unharmed."

"You and me both." Perseus admitted and zipped up his jacket before opening the front door.

The crisp morning mountain air filled his lungs and invigorated his mind. He had come to know the Tatra mountains like the back of his hand, both the outside facade as well as the inner caves and the tunnel's connections. Especially the tunnel connections. Not many were aware of the tunnel network hidden within the mountains. But he was. And he owed that knowledge to Alan. He owed much more to the man, but he chose to accept it rather than dwell on it. Just as he chose to use those tunnels to move about the mountains as a volunteer to save those whose lives hung dangerously close to the edge of life.

This time was no different. A mother, and her three young sons. He was provided with their information, but not their backstory. The backstory always fueled his drive to help those in need. He may have been a loner, but he soon began to find interest in learning about the stories, albeit the short versions, of those he rescued. It wasn't nosiness, nor did it carry an ulterior motive. He simply hoped to one day come across someone whose story may provide a hint that would lead him to finding the truth about his parents' passing.

With that thought far from his mind, though, Perseus arrived at the destination indicated by the dispatcher. He exited one of the caves and found himself at the bottom of a steep mountain cliff-like wall. He looked around and did not come across any sign of the family that had gotten lost. He called the dispatcher and advised her of his arrival. The dispatcher noted the information and advised Perseus the rescue helicopter was on its way, and for him to follow the side of the mountain.

He began to move forward, listening to even the smallest sound he could detect with his ears but most importantly with his mind. Not far from the cave's entrance, he heard a sound that caused him to pause. With his eyes closed, he concentrated on the silence around him. The snow, the mountain breeze, the way the air moved along the mountain. And he heard the sound again. No. He heard... a thought.

His heartbeat quickened its pace and his eyes opened at once. If he heard a thought, then those he was searching for must have been nearby. He closed his eyes again and listened. But what he heard cut through him with such shock he barely reacted as a man's body fell from the cliff of the mountain, landing right at his feet.

The sight of the lifeless body dismayed him, but it was the thoughts Perseus heard a moment before that left him speechless. And without any doubt whatsoever about what he had just witnessed.

'I can't believe father's dead because of me. Now there's no way to save mother...'

≈ Chapter 2 ≈

Never a fan of surprises or unforeseen predicaments, Perseus looked down upon the man whose last breath of life had already been taken and scratched his beard. He sighed heavily, looking up.

Did he suspect whoever stood atop the cliff above could be part of the party he was searching for? The thought did cross his mind. But the more he thought of it, the more questions filled his head. Not regarding the guilt of the person whose thoughts he heard a moment ago, but regarding the reasons behind the man's fall.

He realized, without a doubt, he would have to leave the man where he laid. He would have to resume the search for those who he set out to find, whether they were responsible for the man's demise or not. Sighing heavily, Perseus contacted the search and rescue dispatcher to request for the helicopter to direct its path toward his current location.

"You found them?!?" The dispatcher exclaimed, impressed. "I'm not too surprised since You usually find the wanderers first."

"Well, Ana, then let me surprise You for a different reason. I came across a dead man."

"A dead man?" Ana did not hide the astonishment in her voice. "No one reported that a man went missing?"

"They wouldn't have the time. He dropped dead at my feet," Perseus replied, narrowing his eyes on the man.

"That's not funny."

"It wasn't meant to be. He was alive and kicking when he was falling. No one would have survived that impact."

"What are Your coordinates?" Ana typed the information into the computer database, modifying the data routed to the rescue helicopter.

"There's no area wide enough here for the helicopter to land. The guys will need to drop down from the air."

"Was he alone?"

"Yes." Perseus lied. Revealing his knowledge of those who he did not see atop the cliff was out of the question. Revealing his hidden gift of reading minds, even more so.

"No foul play?"

"No. At least not from where I am standing."

"Mind standing closer?"

"Fine," he sighed and knelt over him to examine the body.

"Well?" Ana inquired, impatient.

"Well, facial recognition is out of the question."

"Not funny."

"Fine."

"Is there any identification on the deceased that could aid in identifying the man?"

"I don't see any. He'll have to be checked out after the guys get here." Perseus realized the man did not fit a profile of someone who would have consciously set out to hike in the mountains. Especially not on a cold December day.

"Anything strikes You as odd or suspicious?"

"He has no hiking boots. No gear either. His suit's fitted for a Christmas dinner rather than mountain climbing. It's as if he wasn't prepared for whatever he was doing up there." Perseus looked up, wondering if those who witnessed the man's fall - or caused it - still stood on higher ground.

It was then that thoughts of a young boy, faint and petrified as they may be, reached him quite unexpectedly.

'How are we supposed to get the antidote now? Mother will not survive without it...'

Those thoughts baffled and alarmed Perseus all the more. Whoever, or whatever, he was dealing with, took on a twist of an utterly different sort. Perseus rose to his feet and knew what needed to be done next. He needed to reach the top of the cliff, and he needed to do so at once.

"Perseus?" Ana repeated his name. "Perseus?"

"Sorry," he shook his head. "There is nothing I can do for this poor man. But there are those who can still use my help - if I'm lucky."

"You mean if they are lucky?" Ana narrowed her eyebrows, intrigued by the choice of words the man she had known for years had used for the first time since they met. Perseus Alexander, as he was known by those who met him in Poland, was not a man who spoke of his luck. Ever.

"You bet." Perseus agreed absent-mindedly. "You've got the coordinates for this location. I'll go on ahead in search of the mother and her kids."

"Alright," Ana understood.

"Ana?" He paused right before resuming the search.

"Yes?"

"Can You do me a favor?"

"What is it?"

"Can You keep me informed if the guys or the coroner find any identification on this guy?" He may have had a habit of figuring out backstories of those he met in the mountains, but this case was different. Not because of the growing sense of intrigue behind it, but because of a tick at the back of his neck. Something did not feel right.

"Another Alexander hunch?" Ana half-grinned but that grin disappeared because Perseus's hunches never led to positive results.

"More like an itch."

"Don't scare me. Those are even worse."

"Hopefully not this time."

"Says a man who doesn't believe in hope."

"I believe in intentions and results."

"Then make sure Your intentions lead to the results we set out for."

"You and me both." He tipped his head, looking up again, and not because he heard the echoing sound of an approaching helicopter in the distance.

"I can hear the rescue team. They are not far. I'll fire the flare so they can have a visual of this location. I'm heading up the mountain."

"Alright. Let me know if You come across any trace of the missing party."

"Will do." The moment he ended the call, he looked down at the man lying at his feet for the last time, and then up towards the cliff from which the man fell, calling out at the top of his lungs.

"Whoever is out there, stay where You are! Don't worry, I'm coming to get You!"

He meant well. Yet the poorly chosen words, albeit harmless and innocent on his part, were received by those up on the cliff as anything but.

'We're doomed now...!'

'He saw us! We must rush mother to safety...!'

Yet the final thought Perseus heard cut through his conscience with an oddly familiar sense of... culpability.

'This never would have happened if it wasn't for me...'

Perseus directed his steps toward the inside of the mountain at once. He was a mountain climber, fast and experienced, but he knew perfectly well that the tunnels within the mountains offered the most efficient paths leading upwards.

The moment Perseus exited one of the caves near the steep mountain cliffside, he called out to whoever he heard before. Again, and again. To no avail. He reached the spot from where he believed the man fell. And all he found was a bunch of blurred, smudged traces of footprints, crushed snow mixed with rocky dirt, and no sight of a living soul.

"Damn." He swore under his breath. "Double damn."

Swearing more profoundly on the inside because of referring to infamous words of one rather famous brother-in-law of his, Perseus grit his teeth, closed his eyes, and listened.

He listened to the wind moving about the tree branches.

He listened to the snow caressing the wintery bushes.

He listened to the difference in the sound ever so detectable between the crushed snow and the untouched snow skimming the ground.

He opened his eyes with a keen understanding of where the missing mother and her children were heading. They were heading toward the Ku Dziurze Gorge. They were heading towards his home. His hidden home. A cabin no one beside Alan was aware of. And he needed to do everything in his power to keep it that way...

Chapter 3

It has often been said by the wise ones of the world that the way home always seems shorter than the path leading away from it. Perseus couldn't agree with such a statement, not in the least. He rushed home at a pace which put his heart into unfathomable overdrive.

Though he ran between the trees, crushing snow under his boots and brushing his knees against the leafless bushes, he could not shake off the ill feeling that his hidden home was about to be exposed - not only by those he was searching for, but also by those who would soon arrive as part of the search and rescue team.

This, ABOVE ALL, he could not allow.

The moment he reached his mountain cabin, he stopped. Stopped and listened, gasping to catch his breath. He listened for any sign of life other than that of the nature surrounding him. He exhaled with frustration. He heard nothing out of the ordinary. The snow still covered most of the ground and shrubs surrounding the homestead. The trees still swayed gently in the late morning breeze. The Ku Dziurze stream still danced around its shallow rocky bed beside the cabin, flowing unbothered down the mountain. It all looked quiet and undisturbed.

Too undisturbed for an Alistair not to become suspicious...

"Double damn." Perseus scratched his beard. It wasn't in his nature to be wrong about the trail he chose to follow during a search and rescue. Nor was it often that his gut proved to be wrong. He grit his teeth and closed his eyes to concentrate better on the surrounding voices. And swore again. "Double damn."

"Tell me about it." Alan caught him off guard as he stood in the cabin's side door, startling Perseus.

"I hate when You do that," Perseus all but growled at the man.

"Do what? Wait for You whenever You take off for a search and rescue?" Alan raised his eyebrow. "Isn't that what friends do?"

"No."

"Oh?" Alan lowered his eyebrow, a bit amused because he understood Perseus's odd sense of humor.

"I didn't mean it that way," Perseus grit his teeth. "Thank You for waiting. I just hate when You catch me off guard."

"I wonder how that could be possible since You can read minds?"

"I read minds. That doesn't mean I can predict what people will do." Saying so, Perseus turned around and around. His growing impatience with not being able to pick up any trace of the mother and her sons he set out to find was getting the better of him. As was his annoyance with himself because of it.

"What are You looking for?" Alan asked, baffled.

"For the mother and her sons."

"Don't tell me they still haven't been found?"

"Fine. I won't." Perseus hissed out, mad at himself for losing their trail.

"Fine." Alan placed his hands on his hips. "But why would You be looking for them here?"

"Because that's where the damn trail led," Perseus hissed out again, looking rather disturbed at Alan.

"Here?"

"Here."

"Are You sure?" Alan grabbed his jacket and closed the door behind him.

"I'm sure. What's worse, the trail leads here and ends here. It just cuts off."

"What could that mean?"

"Either they hid pretty damn well somewhere around here, or I lost the ability to listen."

"Neither of these sound logical."

"I think the world ran out of logic." Perseus crouched down to touch the snowy ground and examined it.

"Care to unpack that for me?" Alan zipped up his jacket.

"I heard them."

"Now?!?" Alan exclaimed, looking around.

"No. Not now," he stood. "Earlier."

"Hmm. So... You found them and heard them but still ended up losing their trail?"

"No. Yes." Perseus nodded. "That's not the worst of it."

"It's not?"

"No. I found them because a man fell down the cliff right by my feet."

"What?!?"

"At least I think it was them."

"Did the man survive?"

"Nope."

"What happened to him?"

"He fell. But I don't think he knew what was happening until it was too late," Perseus moved his shoulders. "But those atop the cliff knew for sure."

"Could he have jumped?"

"I don't think so. I also don't think he anticipated ending up at the bottom of the cliff either."

"Why?"

"Because it didn't look like he was dressed to take on the Tatra Mountains. His suit and tie matched his prim and polished Cap-Toe Oxfords. No one in their right mind would hike the mountains dressed like that - especially this time of the year."

"What do You think led him to that cliff?"

"Apparently whoever I was searching for," Perseus resumed walking around the house. He had to find them. Had to. If he didn't, he would soon have to contact Ana and convince her he was still in a different location and not near his home. Anywhere but his home.

"But why would someone dressed like that come searching for them?" Alan followed Perseus.

"Better question to ask would be why they didn't return to their hotel when they realized he followed them."

"That is definitely a better question. Or a more ominous one. But why would You assume that's why they didn't return to the hotel?"

"Because I heard their thoughts from atop the cliff."

"Double damn," Alan swore loud enough for Perseus to hear it and look back at him. "What?"

"Nothing. I guess it's a day for J.J. Monroe quotes."

"I happen to like the man."

"So do I. But I think I already overused that expression today." Perseus inclined his head toward Alan. "Just don't say it again when I tell You that I think those three sons helped push the man over the cliff because he poisoned their mother."

"DOUBLE..."

"I said don't say it." Perseus pointed at Alan.

"Are You sure You heard what You heard?"

"Did my mind-reading ever fail me?" Perseus replied with a question that twisted a knot somewhere deep inside.

"Never." Alan's response may have satisfied Perseus's ego, but it did not soften the knot in his stomach.

"Exactly." Perseus clicked his tongue. "But that's not all."

"What more could there be? Beyond the notion of foul play from what You already mentioned?" Alan walked toward the edge of the little trail leading toward the stream to see if perhaps the missing party hid on the other side of the holographic walls surrounding Perseus's house area.

"Oh, there seems to be quite a bit of foul play when it comes to this whole thing." Perseus followed Alan to check on the security perimeter. "From what I heard those kids think, the man who fell down the cliff was their father."

"What?!?" Alan turned at once to look at Perseus, and lost his footing, almost falling to the ground. Perseus saved him from falling at the last moment. "They killed their father?!?"

"Yes. For apparently poisoning their mother."

"Triple damn in that case."

"I'll be sure to tell Monroe You one-upped him," Perseus offered him a quick grin which disappeared in an instant.

"What is it?" Alan saw the sudden change in Perseus's eyes.

"Shhh..." Perseus waved his hand to signal for Alan to stay still. "We're not alone."

"Is it them?" Alan whispered, looking in the direction which sparked Perseus's curiosity.

"I sure hope so." Perseus sent his friend a non-verbal queue to stay where he stood and moved slowly toward the shed camouflaged to appear as a large rocky boulder.

"How did they figure out a way to get inside the shed?" Alan's whisper came so unexpectedly behind Perseus it startled him. This surprised Alan even more. "You're off Your game if I was able to catch You off guard."

"You didn't."

"Your sham honesty is worse than Caelum's," Alan shook his head.

"I won't respond to that."

"Exactly," Alan retorted with confidence, but winced as they both heard a crushing sound coming from the shed. He nudged Perseus to quicken his pace.

Perseus did. He rushed toward the hidden entrance of the shed. He opened the door in a swift move after entering the passcode and froze. A woman, clearly unconscious, laid on the floor. Her head rested on the knees of a boy no more than 10 years old. Her hand was held by another boy, slightly older than the first one. But it was the sight of the eldest son that got to Perseus - not because of the boy's fists aimed at him but because of the boy's direct gaze and his whisper:

"Stay away from our mother..."

Chapter 4

Facing an unprecedented opponent, Perseus had to admit that he was... rather impressed. The young man standing before him appeared much braver than his years would indicate. Much bolder. And very much more focused. If Perseus had to guess, he would wager his Alistair mind-reading talent that the young man was the one whose whispers of guilt he heard from atop the cliff.

Was the young man ready to defend the woman lying unconscious on the floor behind him? Yes. Was he willing to accept whatever force Perseus deemed appropriate or necessary in this case? It appeared so. Was he foolishly naive in presuming to stand even the slightest of chances against a seasoned assassin? Evidently, yes...

Though the young man was ready to fight, he underestimated his opponent in one simple yet overly complex way - he concentrated on Perseus's physical strength knowing nothing of his mind-reading aptitude. The young man was about to charge forward to defend his mother, when his words, albeit the unspoken ones, caused Perseus to soften his stance and presumably drop his defenses.

'I lost one parent today; I won't lose another...'

"I must say, to trespass is one thing. To attack the property owner is another." Perseus spoke in a tone of voice that revealed to Alan he was not going to fight.

"I am not attacking You! I am defending my mother and brothers!" The young man's fists went up, but it was his teary eyes that caught Perseus's attention.

"Maybe if You show me more consideration than You did to my property, we could try to help Your mother instead of wasting time throwing punches?" Perseus looked directly into the young man's eyes, which obviously raised the young man's temper.

"There is no way You'll get past me!" The young man hissed out and took a step toward Perseus.

"There is no need to attack us, son," Alan advised the young man.

"Don't talk to me like that! I am not Your son!" The young man shouted at Alan.

"You break into my shed, attack me, then You insult my friend by raising Your voice at him. Your chances of getting out of here just dropped to zero." Perseus frowned. He realized then that he was not facing a scared rival - he was facing a young man who had been hurt by life.

"Stop it, Tristan! Mother needs help!" The boy kneeling beside his mother while holding her hand scolded his brother, causing the young man, Perseus, and Alan to look his way.

"He's right," Alan said first, and walked past Perseus but the young man took a step to the side and blocked Alan's path to the woman lying on the floor.

"How do I know You won't hurt her?" The young man narrowed his eyes on Alan.

"The poison in her blood will do much more damage than us helping her." Perseus said without thinking, immediately biting his tongue.

"How do You know she's been poisoned?!?" The young man gazed back at Perseus with suspicion and astonishment in his eyes. As did Alan.

"She looks poisoned to me." Perseus replied in short. How was he supposed to reply to the question pertaining to his mind-reading ability? Moreover, he was just as taken aback by his own candid revelation of the knowledge of the poison as everyone else was.

"She does." Alan agreed, though he raised his eyebrow at Perseus's blunt mention of the woman's condition.

"But how did You know?" The boy holding the mother's hand repeated the question.

"How did You get inside my shed?" Perseus countered the boy's question.

"My brother is a computer whiz. He figured it out," the youngest boy chimed in in a broken voice without specifying which brother he was implying to. "Can You please help my mama?"

"With Your oldest brother's permission," Perseus replied to the boy and looked at the young man standing in his and Alan's way.

"Fine. But be careful." The young man's stare was meant to come off as an ominous one, but it did little to ruffle Perseus's feathers. He walked between the young man and Alan and knelt beside the mother, facing the younger son. He checked the woman's pulse. He checked her forehead and cheeks, acknowledging her damp yet cold to the touch skin. He then closed his eyes and listened to whatever thoughts may have been running through the woman's mind.

"Are You sure he knows what he's doing?" The young man looked at Alan.

"Perseus is part of the Tatra Volunteer Search and Rescue. He saves people. I would trust him with my own life," Alan replied sincerely, accidentally revealing Perseus's name. "If anyone can save Your mother, it will be him."

"What's Your mother's name?" Perseus sent Alan a scolding gaze of disapproval for revealing his name, and looked back at the young man.

"Andromeda," the young boy replied.

"You don't say?" Alan raised both eyebrows, then bit his tongue when Perseus sent him a blunt stare.

"What's wrong with her name?" The young man scolded Alan.

"There is nothing wrong with Your mother's name," Alan retorted.

"Alan is into Greek mythology," Perseus, too, scolded Alan in an indirect way. "Now, everyone be quiet."

"Why?" The young man asked with suspicion.

"So he can hear her," Alan touched the young man's shoulder, glad the young boy didn't brush off his hand.

"Andromeda?" Perseus closed his eyes again. "Andromeda, can You hear me?"

"Do You think she can?" The young boy asked, but winced when Perseus opened his eyes once more and looked at him while shaking his head, only to close them again.

"Andromeda, can You hear me?" Perseus repeated the question. Not hearing any response, he took hold of the mother's hand, and leaned in. "Can You feel my hand?"

'I need You...'

The woman's weak and barely audible whispers of thoughts stunned Perseus. He opened his eyes at once. "She's still conscious. We need to take her inside the house."

"You're not touching her again!" The young man took a decisive step forward and brought his fists up.

"Your tongue is quicker than Your better judgment," Perseus inclined his head. "Your mother needs help and not force."

"He's right," the younger boy facing Perseus agreed. His words worked because the young man lowered his fisted hands.

"Now, step aside." Saying so, Perseus released the woman's hand only to place his arms under her neck and knees. "Alan, open the doors to the house."

"Alright," Alan nodded. "Boys, follow us."

"Where are You taking her?" The youngest boy asked the moment Perseus rose to his feet with the woman in his arms.

"Inside the house. We need to get rid of the poison in her bloodstream," Perseus noted aloud as he carried her.

"Will she survive?" The younger boy asked as they trudged toward the cabin, with snow creaking under their shoes.

"The sooner we help her, the better the chances for her survival." Perseus explained, pausing because he heard the woman's faint thoughts again.

'I need You...'

"What is it?" Alan caught up with Perseus, worried.

"We need to get rid of the poison, and fast. She's getting weaker." Though he didn't know the woman he carried in his arms, he felt responsible for her wellbeing. Moreover, the woman's silent plea got to him.

"Where are You going to put her?" The eldest son asked as they walked inside the house through the side kitchen door.

"I live alone. There's only one bed where I can lay her down," Perseus explained and took the lead walking toward one of the two open doors at the back of the house. "My bed."

"No!" The eldest son protested, stepping in front of Perseus at the foot of the intricately hand-carved queen-sized bed.

"I think we're past trusting me with Your mother's life," Perseus fired back, impatient with the son's reaction. "You chose to trespass on my property. I chose to help Your mother instead of pressing charges against You. Now, step aside. Each second of delay that passes puts Your mother's life in even more danger."

"Fine." The young man whispered with thunder in his eyes and resignation in his voice.

"I think we need the Survival Kit," Perseus advised Alan as he laid the woman on his bed and unzipped her jacket.

"You do?" Alan asked, alarmed.

"I do. But that's not all."

"What else do You need?"

"I need to get in contact with Gunay and Tom," Perseus replied, utterly discontented about the recent turn of events...

≈ Chapter 5 ≈

Perseus sat on his bed beside the woman he was now entrusted by Fate to save and gazed upon her face with narrowed eyebrows. He felt uneasy, which said a lot about his state of mind because he hated feeling that way. He loathed uncertainty, especially for a mind reader. What he loathed even more was being thrust into a situation beyond his control. Especially after the recent turn of events pertaining to his brother Caelum and their rush against time to save the lives of the woman and child Caelum loved.

Sighing heavily, Perseus removed the woman's jacket and realized there were no exterior signs of her being poisoned, though he knew if he didn't work fast things would turn from bad to worse. He also knew something else. For a mind reader, he had more questions than answers. And it bothered him even more than Alan or any of his siblings would understand.

Was he compelled to save the woman whose long dark hair spread across his pillow? Yes. Was he capable of doing so? Hopefully, with the inevitable use of the 'Alistair Survival Kit' if it would come to that. Was he aware that his siblings would mock him for not finding the woman sooner before she and her sons reached his hidden mountain cabin? Yes. Most uncomfortably yes.

Right... The woman's sons.

Dealing with an unconscious woman was one thing. Dealing with her three sons was another. Not only were they worried about their mother's health, but they were also very suspicious of Perseus and the fact his homestead appeared to be guarded and secured beyond the usual measures would require.

"Are You sure You can save mother?" The eldest son breathed almost at Perseus's neck, standing right behind him.

"Yes," Perseus replied in short.

"Are You sure You can combat the poison in her system?" The young man continued to ask questions.

"Yes." Perseus repeated his previous answer.

"Will You be able to remove it completely, so it won't cause any more damage?" The young man asked, more impatiently.

"I need to neutralize the poison first. Then I'll worry about removing it from her bloodstream," Perseus retorted without looking at him as he checked the woman's vital signs. "Her temperature keeps rising."

"But You know a way to bring it down?" The youngest boy chimed in as he stood in the doorway with tears in his eyes.

"Yes," Perseus looked at the boy. "What's Your name?"

"Kai," the boy replied shyly.

"Kai, You look like a very brave boy. I am sure You all went through a lot in the past few days. I am also sure Your mother would like for You to stay brave for as long as You can." Saying so, Perseus rose from the bed and walked toward the boy standing in the doorway, turning to the eldest son. "Do You have any idea how Your mother was poisoned?"

"No. But she was fine until father caught us on the Mountain cliff, shortly before You found us," the young man said in a lowered tone of voice.

"And You don't know what poison could have been given to her?"

"No," the young man replied, angry with himself.

"Alright," Perseus nodded, then looked back at the youngest boy. "I need to go look for something that will determine what she was poisoned with. Then we'll find an antidote for the poison. Can You stay here with Your brothers and speak to Your mother so she knows You are near her?"

"But she's unconscious." The middle son looked at Perseus skeptically.

"Unconscious people have a way of hearing what is being spoken to them," Perseus inclined his head toward the boy.

"You're just saying it to make us less scared," the boy replied, again with skeptical undertones.

"Yes and no. Trust me," Perseus nodded and began to leave the room when the boy stood in his way.

"Why should we trust You?" The boy tipped his nose up.

"Because I mean You no harm. I am a member of the Tatra Volunteer Search and Rescue. And because You all chose to hide in my shed, not the other way around," Perseus noted with a bit of an authoritative tone of voice, realizing the young boy looking up at him reminded him of himself at that age. "What's Your name?"

"Liam," the boy replied and tipped his nose up again. "And we may have hidden in Your shed, but we won't allow You to take advantage of Our fear."

"You're the one who figured out the lock combination on the shed." Perseus narrowed his eyes on the boy.

"So what?" The boy tipped his nose even higher.

"I'm impressed." Perseus nodded, glad his short answer threw the boy off, eliminating further questions. "Now, I need for You three to stay here and keep Your mother company."

"Yes, Sir," the youngest boy agreed. "Please come back soon."

"Will do," Perseus looked at the three boys, and left the room. He walked to the room on the other side of the kitchen, gesturing to Alan to come join him, then locked the door behind them.

"Are You sure the 'Survival Kit' will be necessary?" Alan inquired as he walked toward the presumably unused fireplace in the room resembling a sparsely furnished home office.

"I'm Alistair sure." Perseus sat behind the heavy hand-crafted wooden desk and reached inside one of the drawers, pressing a barely visible wooden lever which revealed a hidden compartment with the long narrow black wooden box. He opened the box and looked at the linctus vial, picking it up. "I had a feeling this might come in handy again, but I didn't think I'd have to use it so soon, and on someone else again."

"Caelum used his on Anya," Alan noted and pulled a hidden lever on the inside of the unused fireplace, revealing a hidden door that opened on the back wall of the fireplace.

"And I used mine on Caelum," Perseus shook his head. "I'm glad Luna was able to send this one to me when she did."

"I wonder if she will say anything about the high probability of You using another linctus vial so soon."

"You can bet on it," Perseus sighed. "But we don't have much time, and without knowing what poison was used, the woman's life is in danger. We might have no other choice."

"You could try activated charcoal antidote?"

"I don't have time to prepare it."

"Agreed. But do You think contacting Tom and Gunay is necessary?" Alan asked without looking at Perseus while entering a lock combination in the door in the back of the fireplace.

"I'm sure," Perseus closed the desk drawers, returned the chair to its original position, and rose from the desk. "It's not just about the woman and her life. Something doesn't seem right about all of this."

"What do You mean?"

"From what little I learned from the youngest - and from what I deduce the most trusting son - their mother realized their lives were in danger, so she decided they needed to flee from their home on the other side of the Mountains," Perseus walked toward the fireplace and waited for the door to open.

"Did either of the boys say why?"

"No, but I doubt they would know the truth. Andromeda must have found out something bad about their father, and now she's fighting for her life because of it."

"If they traveled from the other side of the Tatra Mountains, especially in this weather, whatever she found out must have been serious."

"And life-threatening." Perseus bowed his head to enter through the door in the fireplace. "Unfortunately for them, someone must have recognized them at the hotel she deemed safe to stay for the night."

"And that someone tipped off the father - which means he had connections she wasn't aware of," Alan replied with anger, so out of character for him it caused Perseus to look at him twice.

"That could be true." Perseus patted Alan's shoulder. "I'll be right back. Make sur to keep those boys occupied, and out of this room. I need to check with Gunay what can be done for the mother."

"And with Tom," Alan added as if on autopilot.

"And with Tom." Perseus agreed, swearing under his breath as he walked through the door and closed it behind him, returning the fireplace to its original appearance...

≈ **Chapter 6** ≈

Activating the wall mechanism in his underground hidden office which set in motion the signal to his two brothers bothered Perseus just as much as acknowledging the simple truth that he was stuck helping total strangers who trespassed his homestead premises without him detecting it.

Was he mad? Yes, but at himself.

Was he unnerved? Yes, because of his inability to catch up with the woman and her sons before they found his home.

Was he stuck? Yes, with consequences of his failed actions.

Swearing to himself prior to his siblings answering the call, Perseus sighed heavily. He screwed up. Big time. And his brothers would surely take notice of it, whether he liked it or not.

"Mountain Boy, to what do we owe the summons?" Gunay smirked with amusement.

"I missed You," Perseus grinned briefly at the monitor with his brother's reflection. "How's São Paulo?"

"Not as cold as Zakopane." Gunay winked at Perseus. "I thought You were on Your way to Isola Bella to spend Christmas and New Years with Caelum and Emmeline?"

"I was," Perseus nodded.

"Knowing Perseus, he probably stayed behind to help in a search for some wandering soul missing in the Mountains," Tom greeted his brothers with a casual wave of a hand as he joined in on the conversation.

"That's right," Perseus agreed.

"And did You find whoever it was You were searching for?" Gunay grinned, sitting behind the sleek and modern glass desk at his São Paulo high-rise penthouse.

"Yes and no." Perseus sighed again, searching for the right words.

"Care to elaborate?" Tom narrowed his eyes. Perseus was a man of few words, but he rarely had a tough time revealing information to his siblings.

"They found me."

"They?" Tom and Gunay said in unison.

"A mother and her three sons," Perseus added, trying his best to remain calm.

"What were they doing in the mountains on Christmas Eve?" Gunay wondered, intrigued.

"Not hiking, if that's what You had in mind. They were fleeing to save their lives."

"From whom?" Tom asked, suspecting a chain of events Perseus would not have been comfortable with. And neither would they since their brother was so secretive about it.

"Apparently from their father."

"Why?" Gunay asked before Tom could speak.

"He wanted to poison the mother." Saying so, Perseus paused his steps for a moment. He recalled the way he felt drawn to the woman when he gazed upon her face as she laid on his pillow. The way it captured his conscience. The way he found it difficult to look away.

"Why?" Gunay repeated his question.

"I don't know," Perseus shook his head, gauging it was best to pretend Gunay asked about the mother's wellbeing and not on his difficulty to look away from her face. "Neither do the sons."

"Can't You ask her?" Gunay inquired further, but Tom didn't have to.

"He can't. The father succeeded with his intention," Tom said quietly.

"Why did You read my mind?" Perseus looked at Tom with anger and resentment. "I didn't give You permission."

"You didn't have to," Tom narrowed his eyes even more, intrigued by his brother's defensiveness. "And neither did I. I did not read Your mind. Your response speaks for itself."

"Fine." Perseus puffed out air. "Anyway, that's the reason for my call."

"What is?" Gunay leaned back in his chair. "To let us know You found a missing party in the mountains? This isn't Your first rodeo, brother."

"Shut up." Perseus scolded him. "I need Your help."

"Damn." Gunay flashed a full-blown smile. "Now THAT'S a first."

"Shut up." Perseus repeated. "I need to figure out what kind of poison the dead guy used to poison the mother."

"Dead guy?" Gunay leaned forward. "I thought You don't stoop so low to our level and dispose of people in hand-to-hand combat, even if the guy did poison her?"

"I don't. I didn't." Perseus stuck his hands in his dark washed out jeans. "The guy fell to his death at my feet."

"Double damn," Gunay leaned back in his chair once more.

"How did You figure out he was the father?" Tom asked but neither brother needed to hear the answer. Then again...

"I heard the oldest son's thoughts. At least I think they were his."

"Oh?" Gunay leaned in even more. "And?"

"And the guy fell because the kid pushed him," Perseus advised them in a much calmer tone of voice than Tom would have expected. Which only meant one thing.

"The kid did it in self-defense," Tom noted matter-of-factly.

"His mother's and his siblings' self-defense." Saying so, Perseus walked out of the room to the adjacent, dimly lit one. He soon returned with a black suitcase, laying it down on the desk, facing the wall of monitors. "This is no match to Your med lab, but it better be enough to save that woman."

"You need to establish two things before finding the antidote," Gunay rose from the desk and retrieved his laptop.

"And those would be?" Perseus opened the suitcase and took out a high-tech microscope along with a slew of other high end medical equipment.

"You need to figure out how the poison was administered to determine the quickest way to administer the cure. And You also need to make sure to transport the woman close enough in distance for You to help her after we figure out what poison was used." Gunay's words did not surprise Perseus. They annoyed him.

"If I knew how she was poisoned, I'd have spared You both the call." Though he raised his voice by a sliver, neither brother mistook it as a coincidence.

"If You needed my help, You could have thought it. I would have heard You," Tom replied in a dry tone.

"You would have. Gunay is a different story," Perseus looked at Gunay and clicked his tongue.

"Ouch." Gunay winced. "Those are some bold words for someone presumably seeking my help."

"Don't flatter Yourself." Tom crossed his arms, switching his stance to a more formal one. "The woman has poison in her blood. You need to work fast, or the poison will overtake all of her organs."

"You'll need to obtain a blood sample and upload the information in the system. The sooner the better," Gunay warned him. "Send me the info and I'll handle it."

"Will do," Perseus inclined his head and grabbed hold of a vial to retrieve a blood sample. "I'll be right back."

"She's at Your place?!?" Tom raised his voice.

"How on green earth did You let them slip by Your state-of-the-art defenses and flashy security system?" Gunay chuckled.

"It's not flashy." Perseus hissed back, aware he had it coming, especially from Gunay. His brother's level of self-absorbed cockiness was only outdone by their other brother Caelum. He also decided it was best not to confront Tom about reading his mind without permission when it came to figuring out the woman's whereabouts.

"And apparently, it's not working either," Gunay chuckled once more, mocking him. "All that work for nothing."

"It wasn't for nothing. And it works just fine," Perseus puffed out a brooding puff of air, admitting defeat. "The woman's kid disarmed the security system and overrode the code to the shed."

"Double damn," Gunay laughed. "The kid not only pushed his father down the mountain to save his mother, but he also outsmarted You? He sounds like an Alistair to me."

"No, that was the other son." Perseus explained, which he knew proved pointless when it came to Gunay.

"There are three sons." Tom finally chimed in. "Keep up with the conversation, Gunay, instead of gloating in Your undefeated glory."

"It's not undefeated." Perseus hit Gunay's ego where it hurt.

"Ouch." Gunay narrowed his eyes, accepting the blow like a champion. "Get me that blood sample. And don't fall for the woman or You'll outshine Monroe and Fin Boy."

"Right. I forgot. I need to let Caelum know I'll be a little late to the party," Perseus scratched the back of his neck.

"I'm sure he won't even notice Your absence with the twins on his hands," Gunay smirked. "Alistair men seem to be dropping like flies."

"You're next." Tom said it so stoically Gunay sent him a blind stare.

"No way. I'm not a kid person." Gunay shivered once more.

"Who said anything about kids?" Perseus grinned at his brother. "Besides, a man like You wouldn't shy away from a challenge now, would he?"

"I live for challenges - just of a different sort," Gunay stretched his arms over his head and linked his fingers, cracking them.

"You and I both," Perseus agreed.

"Got it." Gunay winked. "Just don't make me say I told You so."

"You won't have to." Perseus pointed at him with the empty blood vial.

"Enough chit-chatting. I'll let Caelum know there's been a change in Your plans," Tom grew serious. "You better hurry. Andromeda's condition is worsening."

"Andromeda?" Gunay paused as he began to recline in his office chair, before placing his feet on the sleek glass desk. "My, my, brother. It already looks like I told You so."

"Shut up. You don't have to side with Alan." Perseus retorted, dismissing his brother's statement. "I'll be right back."

"I'll be waiting," Gunay replied with a cocky smile.

And wait for Perseus he did, much longer than he expected. Not out of spite, but because the moment Perseus returned upstairs and rushed to Andromeda's side, he heard her faint repeated plea of a thought as he took hold of her hand to retrieve a sample of her blood.

'I need You...'

Chapter 7

'I need You...'

The thought, barely detectible and ever so delicate, repeated again by unconscious Andromeda, caught Perseus off guard. No. It did not just catch him off guard. It scared him. Why? Heavens only knew. He didn't. At least not at first...

He held his breath, forgetting he was holding her fragile hand in his. He could only stare. He stared at her - her soft and clearly feminine features; her long lashes; her bangs falling along her face as if they were caressing it; her lips. Her lips...

The moment that word formed in his mind, Perseus shook himself back to reality. So much so that Alan noticed it right away. As did the eldest son.

"What's wrong?" The eldest son asked with urgency.

"Nothing's wrong." Perseus replied without looking in the boy's direction. How on earth would he be able to do so after the thought of the mother's lips? How? And then he swore on the inside. How could he - a grown man, no less an assassin - be afraid of a simple gesture of looking someone straight in their eyes?

"Are You certain?" Alan asked as well.

"Certain." Perseus replied in an almost accusatory tone of voice. "I need to draw a sample of her blood to find out what kind of poison was used so I can produce the antidote."

"Are You sure You know what You are doing? You hesitated," the young man took a decisive step forward, standing on the opposite side of the hand-carved bed.

"I did not hesitate. Besides, it's a bit too late for mistrust, don't You think?" Perseus looked at the young man now.

"Our father told us to never trust strangers," the young man said with conviction.

"And where's Your father now?" Perseus regretted asking the question the instant it rolled off his lips. He knew how death of a parent could affect someone. Especially in the case he was dealing with now. Especially because he was aware of the father's Fate even if the sons had no clue that he did.

"He's... hard to get to right now," the young man hunched his shoulders, filled with guilt.

"That's evident." Perseus bit his tongue. He looked at the young man as if they were equals, suddenly cognizant of the young man's necessity to feel important and in charge. "Tristan, may I call You Tristan?"

"Yes, Sir, " the young man nodded.

"Tristan, forget about Your father right now. Forget about what he told You. We need to help Your mother. I will not hurt her. I do not hurt people, I rescue them."

"He's right." Alan approached the young man and laid a hand on his shoulder, glad that Tristan looked down on his hand but did not brush it off.

"Fine. But be professional about it and do it in a way it won't cause her any more harm," Tristan advised Perseus and straightened his back, attempting once more to appear older and braver than his age would indicate.

"You have my word." Saying so, Perseus took a sample of Andromeda's blood with utmost care. The task was simple, and one he had performed hundreds of times, if not more, as a volunteer in the search and rescue. He was good with hands-on aid, even better with administering impromptu on-the-spot assistance in even the worst of cases when someone needed immediate help, but this time he felt oddly uncomfortable drawing blood. Why? He couldn't tell. Was it personal? How could it if they only had met a few hours before. Could he be driven by the unshaken Alistair sense of righteousness to right a wrong? That... he could not deny. What he could do, and this he was certain of beyond any shred of doubt, was to help the woman lying on his bed. A woman who could not ask for help herself. A woman who could not speak up for herself and sons she tried to protect from danger. A woman who crossed the threshold of his homestead. The first and only woman to ever do so. But he dared not focus on that at this moment. "I will be right back."

"Where are You going?" Asked the younger son.

"I will need to examine the blood. I will return with the antidote," Perseus inclined his head toward the boy and turned toward Tristan. "You boys must be starving. My fridge is all but empty as I was heading out of town for a while, but I am sure Alan will be able to prepare something for You."

"That will not be a problem. I got this," Alan smiled at the boys, then looked at Tristan as Perseus left the room. "If it makes You feel safer, how about You and Your brothers take turns keeping watch over Your mother until Perseus finds the antidote? You can take the first turn. I will prepare something to eat and will call You, then Liam or Kai can take Your turn?"

"That does sound better than leaving mother alone," Tristan nodded, sighing a heavy sigh as he rubbed his hands on his face with guilt after the two boys followed Alan to the kitchen.

"How do You feel about a cup of hearty herbal mountain tea?" Alan worked his way around the kitchen, pulling out espresso cups from one of the cupboards. "I hope You will like the tea as much as I do."

"For someone built as tall as Perseus, these cups are tiny." The youngest boy observed with curiosity.

"Perseus prefers his coffee strong. The size of it does not matter as long as it packs a punch," Alan grinned at Kai.

"What's in the other room?" Liam pointed toward the room Perseus walked into, closing the door shut behind him.

"That is his office," Alan explained while he gathered dried herbs for the tea and added them to the teapot, pouring water into the electric kettle.

"Why did he close the door when he walked in there?" Liam inquired further.

"He needs to concentrate on finding the antidote to save Your mother," Alan answered with his face hidden behind the narrow refrigerator door, shaking his head at the clearly empty content of the fridge.

"But why did he lock the door? Is he hiding something?" Liam continued with his line of questions.

"No." Alan replied in short, making sure to hide a smirk at the boy's suspicious nature and clever mind. "Perseus likes privacy. And I hope You boys like bread and wild berries preserves. Perseus ran out of butter, and everything else so it would seem."

"I could eat a whole loaf of bread. I am so hungry," Kai smiled up at Alan.

"I would hold You to that bold admission," Alan grinned at the youngest boy and took out the frozen loaf from the freezer to thaw. "But I am afraid You will need to share the loaf of bread with Your brothers."

"Yes, Sir," Kai agreed with a child's trust in his eyes.

"I am sure Your brothers will be grateful for Your generosity," Alan winked at the boy. "I will bring more food tonight."

"Why?" Liam asked, more suspicious than before.

"Well, for one, Your mother is in no shape to be wandering down the mountains, or out of this house for that matter. And second, Perseus wasn't lying when he said the refrigerator was empty."

"Do You think we will have to stay here for a long time?" Kai sat on one of the hand-crafted wooden stools by the table and looked out the window.

"That would all depend on how soon Your mother can recover," Alan explained as he poured the boiling water into the teapot. "Besides, Perseus will find the antidote, however if Your mother requires further assistance then she may need to be transported to the hospital and You may need shelter until she will heal completely."

"No!" Liam exclaimed in protest.

"No?" Alan looked at him, taken aback by the boy's sudden refusal.

"No." Liam replied, repeating his answer in a calmer yet still firm tone of voice.

"Was that an opposition to Your mother being transferred to the hospital? Or to You staying here?"

"Both," Liam tipped his nose up. "Mother will get better soon. She will not require medical assistance. And we most definitely will not require staying here any longer than necessary."

"As You wish." Alan inclined his head at the boy's fierce gaze. He was about to ask Tristan if the young man wished for his tea to be brought to the bedroom when Perseus flung the office door wide open with an undeniable sense of urgency. He rushed to the bedroom sending an alarmed look Alan's way. "What is it?"

"She needs help! Now!" Perseus offered no further explanation. He did not have time. He rushed to Andromeda's bedside, took her in his arms, and administered one life-saving linctus vial. And hoped to high heavens it wasn't too late...

≈ Chapter 8 ≈

For a man who chose a life of rescuing people from sheer doom in the steep heights of the Tatra Mountains to counteract his 'other' occupation, holding the rescued person who was regaining consciousness usually brought Perseus relief. For an introverted assassin who chose to refuse any and all forms of human contact aside from the bare minimum, holding the woman in his arms felt like anything but relief. It felt odd. It felt intimidating. It felt... ominous.

His first instinct was to let go of the woman. But he couldn't. He was not a coward. So, then, why did his gut turn into knots the moment a set of indescribably deep brown eyes fluttered open and looked up at him?

His second instinct was to swear. Aloud. J.J. Monroe would have referenced the Alistair brothers' uncensored trait if he saw him now, and he... would have been right. But Perseus knew better than to reveal his thoughts to those around him. Especially to the woman's sons.

So, he did the only thing he could do. He held onto the woman, making sure she felt safe in the circumstances she had awoken to.

"Andromeda?" Perseus asked, because everything aside from her name escaped his mind. It was a safe question to ask. At least he thought so. Then again...

'Oh, my stars...'

The sudden thought that formed in the woman's mind surprised him as much as the deep abyss of her eyes. Not because of what she thought, but because he thought the same exact thing at the same exact moment. For more than the obvious reasons...

"Mama!" The woman's younger sons rushed to sit beside her on the other side of the bed, while Tristan hadn't moved an inch from where he stood.

"You are here..." The woman sighed in a weak yet relieved tone of voice.

"We all are mama!" Kai took hold of the woman's hand and hugged it. "And we're safe!"

"We are?" The woman asked, distraught from the pain she felt all over her body and the fact she could barely move - not because of the undeniable grip of strong arms around her but because of the clear understanding the poison she was injected with had worked.

"You are, my dear. You are," Alan advised her with a sincere smile and what looked to be a seasoned gentleman's bow.

"Who are You?" The woman inquired with suspicion as she looked at Alan, hoping to high heavens they were no longer in danger they were running away from.

"My name is Alan." Alan inclined his head. "And the man who carried You here is Perseus."

"You... carried me?" Her voice cracked, causing Perseus's heart to drop a beat.

"You... could say that." Perseus nodded, swallowing hard. He was trapped. He felt trapped. And he was powerless against the odd sensation of losing his footing whilst sitting atop his own bed. It wasn't just the woman's voice. It wasn't her deep brown eyes. It wasn't the sight of the darkened veins painted vividly against the pale skin of her face. It was... a combination of it all.

"He did! Perseus carried You! I saw it!" Kai chirped with joy now that his mother had awoken.

"Didn't I tell You that... You should speak to strangers with respect?" Andromeda scolded her youngest son with motherly concern, taking a labored sigh. "That is Mr. Perseus for You."

"He said we can call him Perseus," Kai replied bashfully.

"He did." Tristan and Liam agreed.

"I did." Perseus shrugged. "How are You feeling?"

"Alive." She tried to smile but winced instead.

"That's a good sign, my dear." Alan advised her, standing behind Tristan.

"What is?" She chuckled lightly. "Wincing from pain?"

"Yes. Wincing from pain means You feel it," Alan explained.

"How could that be good?" Liam wondered with suspicion.

"Since Your mother feels the pain, it means the poison gave way to the antidote and her body is no longer succumbing to the numbness." If Alan had to describe everyone's reaction to his words, he'd have sworn Perseus's surprised him the most. Or rather, his lack of reaction. Perseus neither moved, blinked, nor breathed for that matter. He only stared at the woman being held in his arms.

"Antidote?" Andromeda looked up at Perseus with fear in her eyes. "You... knew I was poisoned?"

"He guessed it because of how You looked," Tristan spoke up, forcing his voice to come off as calm. "He was right, and it shows in how You look now."

"How I look now?" Andromeda asked with worry. "And how do I look now?"

"Better," Perseus said in short.

"Better?" She looked up at Perseus again. "How bad did I look before?"

"Bad." Tristan replied and stuck his fists into the pockets of his jeans. He may have been young, but fury, anger, and guilt filled his veins the same way as it would have if he were older.

"Bad?" She asked, looking from one son to another.

"Bad." Perseus repeated after Tristan. He, too, felt a wave of emotions. And the only thing he was grateful for was that he possessed the ability to read minds of those around him - not the other way around. Otherwise, he'd have a very hard time explaining why his mind was filled with thoughts matching Tristan's.

"Then I must thank You for saving me. For saving us," Andromeda smiled briefly. She meant it as a polite gesture, but it backfired. Right in her face.

"Damn..." Perseus sighed. That - understandably - backfired. In his face.

"Excuse me?" Andromeda blinked with disapproval, narrowing her eyes. "There is no reason to be disrespectful."

"I'm not." Perseus swallowed hard.

"My dear, my friend just saved Your life. He spent hours looking for You. I hope You will understand the strain it caused him." Alan tried to save the situation. "He is quite exhausted."

"He really did save You, mama." Kai squeezed Andromeda's hand.

"Why were You searching for me?" She asked with fear.

"Perseus is a volunteer with the Tatra Mountains Search and Rescue," Alan explained with a nod. "We are all glad You are feeling better."

"Alright," she replied but chose to end the embrace she found herself in. "Would You please let me go?"

"No." Perseus uttered against his better judgment. The blunt response caused Alan to bite his lip in an effort not to chuckle and caused Andromeda to gaze up at Perseus in a way that shot spikes of something unfamiliar at the small of his neck.

"Why not?" She asked, narrowing her eyes on him.

"You're too weak to leave," he said bluntly.

"It was not my intention to leave. I merely asked to be released from Your harsh grip," she explained, doubting why she needed an explanation to begin with. "And please believe me when I tell You that I do not take being called weak lightly."

"You were poisoned. You are weak. And... as You wish," Perseus hissed out, setting the woman he begged the high heavens to survive just a moment ago on his pillow. And wondered why her presence bothered him so much...

≈ **Chapter 9** ≈

What could be said of life's twisted paths? Andromeda Angelis could write a book about the journey her feet led her through her life up until the moment she lost all touch with reality after being poisoned by her husband. The man she thought she could trust...

She used to lead a normal life - if living in over 20 European countries up until age 20 could ever qualify as a normal life. For her, a carefree unattached life equated to such because of one night that forced her to grow up. Barely sixteen, she matured in a heartbeat the night her parents and grandparents lost their lives in a house explosion no one had expected. Bruised and injured, she was told by those attempting to comfort her that although gas explosions weren't common, they did occur, and that she should have considered herself lucky for surviving the blast. She did not feel lucky. On the contrary. She felt far from it. And the guilt of that night laid deep in her heart.

So, she chose to move from one place to another. Leave no trace behind. Leave no friends behind. Leave no roots behind. Until the day she met her future husband. Stoyan Natan was a worldly businessman, eager to find a mother for his young son. A soft spoken yet confident man, smooth around the edges he worked hard to hide from the world. A man who turned out to be so determined in protecting the secrets of his double life that he deemed taking the life of his wife and mother of his children a mere precautionary measure...

"I see You are awake, my dear?" Alan's soft voice brought Andromeda's thoughts back to reality. "I trust You have rested well?"

"Yes." She nodded. "Thank You for allowing me to do so."

"You are most welcome." Alan offered her a kind smile. "An uninterrupted rest does good for the soul - and for the body."

"I am grateful to You for taking care of my children as I slept," she tilted her head, moving up against the single yet oversized pillow behind her back.

"It was my pleasure. I miss the way youth livens up a room. Without them life oftentimes seems desolate."

"I must agree." She nodded. "I hope my boys haven't caused too much trouble."

"Not at all."

"Not even for that man with the angry gaze in his eyes?"

"Perseus? He... can be rough around the edges, but that gaze of his softens over time." Saying so, Alan moved from the doorway and came closer, to sit at the edge of the bed. "I hope You did not take the way he treated You to the heart."

"I did not. Though, I must admit it felt personal," she explained with a heavy sigh, followed by a wince due to pain somewhere deep within.

"It was... personal. Though, not the way You assume," Alan shook his head. "It became personal to him the moment he realized You had been poisoned."

"It did? Why? I am but a stranger to him."

"That may be so. But..." Alan cut his words short, looking back to ensure Perseus would not hear the rest of what he was about to say.

"But?" She asked, puzzled.

"But You are first and foremost a mother. And he knew he'd be damned if he allowed Your boys to lose You." Alan whispered, checking again to ensure they were alone.

"Why?"

"Perseus... lost his mother long ago." Alan leaned forward and laid his hand gently atop hers in a sign of sincerity. "That sort of pain does not go away, even if Fate turns the virtues of life around."

"What does that mean?" She asked, no longer just puzzled, but intrigued as well.

"It means I lost my mother. And since You trespassed on my property, that made it my business to ensure You lived long enough to walk out of here on Your own two feet," Perseus announced his presence in the coldest tone of voice imaginable.

"You're back?" Alan rose from the bed to face Perseus, startled by his sudden appearance.

"Back." Perseus replied without looking at his friend, keeping his direct gaze on the woman lying in his bed. "You're up."

"All thanks to You." Andromeda greeted him in the same cold tone of voice, forcing Alan to bite his lip to hide the urge to smirk. He hadn't met many people who ruffled Perseus Alistair's feathers. Andromeda managed to do so effortlessly.

"Up and strong enough to carry out a conversation, I see." Saying so, Perseus walked toward the bed, placing the backpack he had been holding at Andromeda's feet. "These should fit You."

"What is this?" She blinked twice, once at the clothes and then at Perseus. "I did not ask for anything."

"I know. But You need a change of clothes until You can leave." Though Perseus used a harsh tone of voice, she could find no fault in his words. Then, again...

"What makes You think that I... that we will stay here?" She countered his statement.

"You were poisoned. You won't last in this weather. The snow is coming in pretty heavy by now. And did I mention You won't last in this weather because You were poisoned?"

"And they say chivalry is dead." She mocked him. "As You wish, we will stay here for now."

"Good." Perseus nodded, not entirely pleased with her response. "Look through the clothes. Something in there should fit You. I got some clothes for Your sons as well."

"You did not have to spend money on us," she protested.

"I didn't." Perseus began to turn around to walk out of the room. "Keep what You want out of those. The undergarments are new."

"Thank You," she inclined her head.

"Alright." Perseus sent her a quick look and walked out of the room.

"How soon would You say that gaze of his will turn less threatening?" She wondered, gesturing for Alan to pass the backpack to her.

"When he'll no longer fear You," Alan smiled.

"Fear me?" She scoffed. "I would think it's the other way around."

"Trust me." Alan checked once more to see if Perseus had walked away far enough not to hear him. "He is a caveman, no doubt about it. He keeps to himself, and speaks little, but he is a good man. He saw something in You that cut at his conscience, that's why he's afraid."

"I doubt he saw anything in me other than a nuisance," she whispered, cognizant of Alan's intention to keep their conversation private.

"Fate is quite fickle, my dear," Alan shook his head. "Have You considered the idea You were meant to find Your way to this place?"

"If You are referring to me being poisoned as the prerequisite to meeting that brooding brute who just left, then I refuse to believe it," she noted in a witty way and checked the contents of the backpack.

"If You say so." Alan grinned. "Anyway, I will leave You to see if You can find something in there You may decide to wear. I will tend to Your sons."

"Where are they? It is too quiet here for me to believe they aren't causing any mischief," she noticed suddenly.

"They are outside. There is a snowstorm approaching. They are helping Perseus with securing the homestead and the shed You all hid in," he explained and paused at the doorway. "You are fortunate to have found shelter when and where You did. I hate to sound negative, but whoever poisoned You did not mean You well."

"I'm afraid You are right," she sighed, rubbing at her heart.

"Worry no more," Alan reached for the doorknob. "Perseus may be a brute, as You said, but there isn't a bone in my weathered and seasoned body that would believe he would allow anyone to harm You."

"Even when he just met me and my boys?"

"Yes. That's part of his charm." Saying so, Alan closed the door, giving Andromeda much-needed privacy. And it was good that he did, because it allowed her to keep a reaction of what happened next all to herself.

No one heard her gasp. No one saw her gaze all around the room in disbelief and confusion. No one found it unimaginably impossible when she heard a faint voice within her own thoughts. A man's voice. A masculine voice. A voice that captured her undying attention. Perseus's voice.

'Please, please let her be alright...'

≈ Chapter 10 ≈

Standing on the porch of his cabin facing the Ku Dziurze stream, watching as the setting sun bid farewell to the day with its last rays of December sun, Perseus contemplated the day's events.

The day began with his usual cup of espresso and rays of the same sun caressing his face. Though now, the sun shone in a completely different way. So utterly foreign and different.

It wasn't just the sun that struck Perseus as different. Everything else seemed different, too. His mountain home. The air. Heck, even Alan seemed different to him. Not because the man treated unexpected tenants of the house as welcomed guests. No. Perseus felt that way because Alan seemed to cope very well with the fact they weren't leaving anytime soon - whether he liked it or not.

"You're brooding." Alan joined Perseus on the porch with a freshly brewed cup of strong earthy tea in hand.

"Could be." Perseus shrugged, noticing the steam lifting from Alan's cup. "You, on the other hand, are smiling."

"Could be." Alan's grin widened. "I have my reasons for it."

"Oh, I'm sure of it." Perseus clinked his cup to Alan's cup of tea. "Mind sharing?"

"Since when do You ask to share my thoughts? From what I recall, I have not kept them from You."

"From what I recall, You've never played Mr. Hospitality either, but You seem to have taken an instant liking to our new guests." Perseus chuckled, with more sarcasm than amusement.

"Living like a mountain man clearly affected Your virtue of selflessness." Alan took a few steps forward, placing his hands on the snow-covered porch railing. "I tend to help those in need."

"And what do You presume they are in need of?" Perseus gestured toward the inside of the house.

"Well. Although there is no doubt they all need shelter for the next few days, You have to consider Andromeda's needs would be different from those of the boys."

"What do You mean?"

"They have been through a lot. Andromeda needs to heal, so her needs are more of the physical sort," Alan explained, rolling a handful of snow from the railing into a small snowball. "But those boys? It looks like they are down one parent. You of all people should know what effect it has on someone."

"Yeah." Perseus clenched his jaw at the memory of the day he found out his parents perished years ago.

"Each of those boys understands what happened in a different way. Tristan is filled with worry for his mother because of her being poisoned. He's also filled with guilt because of what happened to his father - and keep in mind they do not know You are aware of what happened on that mountain."

"That kid will do fine," Perseus replied with conviction.

"Did You? Did all of You?" Alan threw the snowball, nodding with approval when the snowball flew across the field in front of the house, flying through the cloaked wall Perseus had installed to keep the tourists away from the house.

"That was different," Perseus protested.

"Of course, it was. You weren't responsible for Your parents' deaths," Alan explained, rolling another handful of snow into a snowball.

"Yeah, well. They didn't die back then after all, did they?"

"But none of You knew that. Tristan knows what he did," Alan threw the second snowball in the same direction, satisfied with his aim. He placed his hand on Perseus's shoulder, turning toward him. "I may be just an old friend, and it may be the winter of my wisdom years talking, but those boys - especially Tristan - need someone to talk to. Someone they would not need to fear. Someone who has no motive other than helping them."

"I don't do well with personal relations. Ask Caelum," Perseus grinned, but the grin disappeared. "Can't I just tolerate them being here until they leave?"

"That choice would be up to You. However, do keep in mind that kindness returns in kindness. They may not be able to offer You anything now, but Fate's Fickle. You may end up owing Your life to them one day." Alan turned to go inside the house, when the doors opened, and Kai popped his head out of the doorway with Liam right behind him.

"Did You need anything?" Perseus looked at them, intrigued.

"May we... play in the snow?" Liam asked with hesitation.

"What?" Perseus wondered, surprised.

"May we please play in the snow?" Kai repeated his brother's question.

"I... guess so," Perseus agreed. "But You have to put on Your coats and boots first."

"Thank You!" The boys smiled, disappearing inside the house only to rush out of it as if it were a race.

Perseus looked at them, smiling. Then he noticed Alan's grin. "What?"

"Nothing." Alan moved his shoulders.

"It's never *nothing* when You have that look on Your face."

"Oh, it is nothing. Unless You figure that You talking to those boys as if it was second nature and then smiling at it amounts to something."

"I don't know what You mean."

"Alright," Alan chuckled. "May I suggest something?"

"No."

"Then I will." Alan chuckled more brightly, aware of Perseus's dry sense of humor.

"Fine." Perseus sighed, resigned.

"You are the man of this house," Alan began, but Perseus shot him a quick look.

"What does that have to do with anything?"

"Everything." Alan took a step toward Perseus to ensure the boys who played in the snow did not hear them. "Do You know what day today is?"

"The day I should have left for Caelum's place in Isola Bella?"

"Some would say You aren't as funny as You think," Alan reprimanded him. "Today is Christmas Eve."

"I knew that."

"Did You?" Alan frowned. "There is no sign of a Christmas tree inside Your cabin."

"If memory serves me, I was on my way to visit Caelum. Did You not notice the empty refrigerator?"

"I did." Alan agreed. "But it would seem life made different plans for You."

"What are You implying?"

"Put the Christmas tree inside until they leave. Make it a surprise. Give those kids a moment they can forget about the cruelty of the world, if even for that one moment." Saying so, Alan rolled a handful of snow, throwing it in the boys' direction. It landed at Liam's feet. Both boys looked at Alan and Perseus. Alan raised his hands up, shaking his head.

"That was unfair! We weren't looking!" Kai exclaimed happily. He crouched down, rolled a snowball, and threw it. The snowball landed with perfect precision - right at Perseus's chest."

"Sorry, Sir!!!" Kai shouted, running toward Perseus, pleading for forgiveness with fear in his eyes. "I didn't mean it."

What caught Perseus off guard was not the boy's sincerity, but the panic filling his young heart. Had the boys not been loved with a father's love? Did they not know how to play without punishment? Could they have gone through life with more trepidation than affection allotted in childhood? Perseus looked at the boy with eyes that softened in a way Alan could not help but notice. Alan also realized Perseus read his thoughts, shooting Alan a gaze that would have scared any other man facing an assassin. But Alan only smiled. Which resulted in a resigned sigh on Perseus's part.

"It would appear You have a strong right arm," Perseus spoke after a moment of silence.

"Tristan taught us." Liam explained as he joined his brother, standing beside him, though with a foot in front of Kai, as if he were protecting his brother.

"Then I would say he taught You well." Perseus nodded with approval. "But I must tell You that I am a professional when it comes to snowball battles."

"He is." Alan agreed, pointing at him.

"What would You say about a snowball fight?" Perseus passed the empty cup to Alan. "But if I win, I get to tell You what Your punishment will be for throwing that snowball at me."

"Deal." Kai smiled shyly, with Liam relaxing his stance.

"You... are not mad at him?" Liam asked with hesitation.

"Why would I be?" Perseus shook his head. "I would have been mad if the snowball landed on Alan."

"Why?" Both boys asked.

"Because he doesn't know how to throw snowballs. If he played on my team, we'd surely lose." Perseus smiled, clicking his tongue. "Now, go out there and start making snowballs. We only have a few minutes before the sun goes down."

"Thank You, Sir." Kai said, a bit less frightened. "I really am sorry."

"I know. I can see it. And that's what matters." Perseus patted his back before the boys ran back to their respective hand-made snow forts.

"What do You think about the punishment for that boy?" Alan wondered once he ensured the boys could not hear them.

"You told me to get a Christmas tree, right?"

"Right," Alan agreed.

"Well, I don't really have any ornaments for that tree. I guess we'll have to make some tomorrow. "Perseus's smirk grew, and his stance softened as he walked toward two boys who could not hide their appreciation for the man who allowed them to stay at his house for the time being. And they weren't the only ones filled with appreciation, for there was someone who heard his thoughts. Even if he wasn't aware of it...

≈ Chapter 11 ≈

It's been said history repeated itself. Perseus laughed that notion off as soon as it formed in his mind. When in the world did he ever chop down a tree on Christmas morning? Or ever before, to be more precise? Not that he didn't understand or observe the holiday in the past. He stopped observing it after Jane and Richard Alistair lost their lives in the line of the proverbial duty. Or rather, after they disappeared from the Alistair siblings' lives.

After all, what was there to celebrate? Loneliness? Sorrow? Betrayal?

There was never a question in Perseus's mind or in the minds of his siblings that whatever happened to their parents was a result of a stab in the back. But why? Was it caused by someone's jealousy? For personal gains? For a corrupt second bottom government's convenience?

Even with Emmeline Alistair's knowledge of the events that followed their presumed deaths, Perseus felt there were too many missing pieces they had not yet uncovered. His parents were heroes, fighting for the righteous side of the law. He was convinced of it. Not because of a child's blind faith in his parents. No. He was convinced of it because of the way his parents raised him and his six siblings, the way they spoke of integrity, the way they spoke of always doing the right thing.

Such as it were, Perseus ended up following the lead of his siblings when they could no longer pretend they would survive by sticking together. They knew they couldn't. It wasn't for the lack of trying. But the more time passed, restlessness and despair took over and each Alistair went in a separate direction. True,

Tom took Luna and Rasalas under his wings as he settled in Cathedral Cove in New Zealand. But it backfired in a tremendous way. Rasalas left Tom's side after falling for the wrong woman thereby almost exposing their identities. And Luna left right before he did. She was torn between doing the right thing following Tom's hunch in saving Rasalas's life, and Rasalas's resentment toward them for it...

And now, years later, as crazy as it felt to him, Perseus was chopping down a Christmas tree at first break of dawn on Christmas Day. The moment the Christmas tree fell to the ground, Perseus cursed Alan out with a hefty dose of brotherly love for coming up with the idea of surprising Andromeda and her sons. Though he considered it a wild idea to begin with, he was soon facing an even bigger dilemma he hadn't thought of before. How in the world would he bring the Christmas tree inside, quiet enough not to awaken anyone, before they woke up? A ruined surprise was no surprise after all...

"Good morning." Andromeda's gentle whisper startled Perseus so much he almost dropped the Christmas tree while trying to secure it in the tree stand he had built shortly before bringing it inside.

"Damn." His reply, although fitting the circumstances, did not impress her.

"Merry Christmas to You, too." She crossed her arms at her chest while leaning on the door's threshold for balance.

"Yeah." That short retort did not impress her either.

"Did You bring that Christmas tree for us?"

"No." Perseus shook his head, realizing instantly it wasn't his usual first line of defense to lie - especially about something as innocent as a guilty-of-nothing tree.

"No?"

"No." He repeated, searching in his mind for anything that could back up his reply. Even if it was another lie. "I always get a Christmas tree on Christmas morning."

"Always?" She nodded as if aware of his poor attempt at a cover up, a bit amused at the questionable way he could not hold eye contact.

"Yes."

"Alright." She walked up slowly to the tree, touching its needles. "If You'd like, I can help You with decorating it. Can You bring the ornaments?"

"No." Was it the panic in his voice that scared him more than it surprised her? He couldn't tell. All he knew was that the explanation he would offer next was finally an honest one. "Your sons will decorate it."

"My... sons?" She whispered, pausing as she caressed the branches of the freshly cut tree. She inhaled its wonderful piney scent and sent him a puzzling look. "But what will they decorate it with? I don't see any boxes of ornaments laying around here?"

"They will make the decorations."

"Make them out of what?"

"Wood, paper, and strings." Saying so, he checked once more that the tree stood securely in its stand and began to retrieve his hands when Kai stood at the doorway of the bedroom with Liam right behind him. "Good morning."

"Good morning." Kai smiled shyly at the sight of the Christmas tree basked in the rays of the morning sun shining through the kitchen window. "Does this really mean we must help decorate it?"

"Yes." Perseus brushed the remainder of snow mixed with pine needles from his winter coat. "I kept my end of the deal."

"What deal?" Andromeda looked from her sons to Perseus.

"We lost a snowball battle." Liam brooded.

"So, decorating the Christmas tree would be considered a form of owning up to our defeat." Kai nodded, as if admitting to a loss in a real battle and walked up to join his mother.

"Is that so?" Andromeda smiled, embracing her youngest son.

"Yes," Kai agreed wholeheartedly. "But we gave our word, so now we have to keep it."

"That, You did." Perseus straightened up, pretending to wince as he touched the place on the chest where a snowball initiating last night's battle had hit him. "Let's just hope Your ornament making skills are gentler than Your aim."

"He hurt You?" Andromeda raised her eyebrows, immediately bringing her hands around Kai, as if shielding him.

"Not entirely." Perseus smiled, cognizant at once that the situation required him to trudge lightly. "But I fully admit my ego suffered greatly."

"But You won the snowball battle?" Liam defended his brother and walked up to stand beside Kai.

"Yes. But Your brother won the first strike because of the element of surprise," Perseus rubbed his chest again.

"I did not mean to aim at You." Kai admitted with guilt.

"I'll be sure to tell Alan he was Your target of choice." Perseus clicked his tongue, smiling wider as Alan walked in. "Speaking of the poor guy."

"Merry Christmas." Alan greeted everyone and removed his hiking backpack and another duffel bag off his back, setting them down by the electric fireplace in the kitchen. "Anyone mind explaining why I'm the poor guy?"

"Believe it or not, but Kai confessed again that he was aiming at You with that first snowball," Perseus grinned at his best friend and crossed the kitchen to help Alan.

"Did he?" Alan sent the boy a joyful nod. "Then You must work on Your aim. I don't move fast these days. I should not be that hard to miss. What do You say we practice some more of that aim of Yours later today?"

"Yes, Sir." Kai smiled with excitement, then looked up to his mother. "Can I?"

"As long as You take Your brothers with You," Andromeda turned toward Tristan who stood in the bedroom's doorway for a long while without saying anything. "Merry Christmas."

"Merry." Was all Tristan said.

"Would You mind spending some time with Alan, Kai, and Liam outside? To make sure they act properly?" Andromeda asked him in a gentle way.

"Sure." Tristan agreed, and Perseus noticed the restraint in his voice. Though others might not have picked up the meaning of the look Andromeda sent Tristan, Perseus understood the unspoken thread linking the mother and her son. A thread of comprehension of what Tristan did to save her life.

"Then I guess we should start on the decorations for this grand example of a scrawny Christmas tree." Perseus said and cleared his throat, hoping to switch the subject to a less burdensome one.

"It is a beautiful Christmas tree. There is nothing scrawny about it." Andromeda shook her head at his description. "But I guess it will look brighter with some hand-made decorations."

"You are correct, my dear." Alan reached down to his backpack, retrieving bags of folded clothes. "I brought some more clothes for the boys. They should fit nicely, I hope. And since yesterday's defeated team will be busy with decorating the tree, maybe You can oversee the culinary portion of today's activities? If You are well enough?"

"Absolutely," she agreed. "My snowball throwing skills are too poor to even mention, but my cooking skills are second to none."

"We'll see about that." Perseus blurted out without thinking. He thought of Rasalas, but Andromeda's ice-cold stare left no question in his mind that she took it personally.

"Challenge accepted." She responded with a straightened back and walked inside the bedroom to find something to change into.

"Let's change, too." Kai nudged Liam, and followed Andromeda, closing the door behind them.

"Do You not know how to speak in the company of others? Especially when speaking to a guest in Your own house?" Alan spoke wondered when they were alone in the kitchen.

"Of course, I do."

"So then let me ask You... were You going to just casually admit to them that Your assassin brother Rasalas's cooking is second to none?"

"No." Perseus brooded, silently admitting Alan was right.

"Then I suggest You figure out a way to change Andromeda's mind about Your lack of manners."

"Fine. How do I do that?"

"By softening the mother's heart in her." Saying so, Alan walked up to one of the cupboards, and reached inside it, retrieving a box filled with herbs and spices necessary for preparing the dinner he had in mind for later in the evening.

"And how do You suppose I do that?" Perseus crossed his arms at his chest.

"By surprising them with unexpected presents under the tree tonight," Alan replied without looking at his best friend, fully conscious of Perseus's glaring stare in his direction...

≈ Chapter 12 ≈

Leaning back in his chair in the high-tech underground office, Perseus looked at the monitors displaying his siblings. Some were alone, some with their families. The world may have been getting ready to celebrate New Year's Eve. But not Alistairs. They were simply enjoying their down time. Albeit, in many different parts of the globe.

Tom Alistair, for one, being the eldest and most stoic of their bunch, did not celebrate the holidays. It wasn't in his blood, so to speak. And it definitely wasn't in his nature. Gunay and Rasalas relaxed on a private beach near São Paulo in one of Gunay's secluded beachfront retreats. As for others? Others found the end of the year to be a time to celebrate how finding love changed their lives in the most inexplicable ways.

Perseus grinned, watching his baby sister Luna as she beamed with a happy second pregnancy glow while J.J. Monroe walked around their office room of their Boston mansion with his sleeping son Caelum 'Seven' Monroe nestled cozily in his arms. If Perseus had to admit, he could have sworn Luna was born to be a mother. And her motherly relationship with J.J.'s daughter Aurora was an example of it in every way possible.

But it wasn't Luna who impressed Perseus. Nor was it Rigel, who had welcomed his newborn daughter Seraphina not long ago. It was actually his brother Caelum who impressed Perseus the most. Why? Because the man simply melted into a heartwarming parental puddle whenever he gazed upon his children. All his children...

"Would You look at Fin Boy?" Perseus called on his brother, which resulted in Caelum turning toward the monitor holding his newborn son. "Not a shred of cockiness left in You, is there?"

"I know, right?" Caelum's eyes gleamed with a father's pride as he cradled little Atlas even more lovingly, forgoing his usual arrogant comeback.

"I would not be so sure," Emmeline chuckled. She walked toward Caelum and handed their newborn daughter to him.

"Me neither." Little Anya chirped happily and took the opportunity to reach for Caelum, only to be picked up by Emmeline. "Papà is a mischief."

"He is?" Perseus chuckled at Anya's directness.

"I agree," Emmeline shook her head with amusement. "But we love him more because of it, don't we?"

"We do!" Anya agreed wholeheartedly.

"Yes, we do." Perseus smiled and turned his attention to Rigel. So much had changed in their lives in such a short period of time. All for the better, even if so much was still yet to be uncovered regarding their parents' disappearance. "Happy Anniversary, Mr. and Mrs. Happyski."

"Thanks, brother." Rigel saluted him casually, gazing back at his wife sitting in the oversized blue chair in the dimmed light of the room filled with dozens of antique lamps in Luna's old apartment, with their daughter nestled cozily in her lap. "You better enjoy those newborn nap times Fin Boy. They do not last. Ask Jade. She takes naps whenever Seraphina snoozes off, and it's less and less often."

"No, they do not last for sure. But those giggles and coos are just as gratifying," J.J. added with pride.

"So are drinks on the beach." Gunay clinked his glass of whiskey with Rasalas's while enjoying the low tide and evening breeze on the private beach.

"Enjoy, gentlemen. But do watch for that laptop," Perseus leaned back in the chair. "It's worth more than those drinks."

"Not on my watch," Gunay clicked his tongue. "I always splurge when I pick my poison."

"I second that motion." Rasalas smirked. "Anyway, how are Your guests doing? I doubt they are singing praises of Your warm hospitality."

"It's not that bad." Perseus grimaced, feeling uneasy as the attention of the conversation turned on him.

"I'll say." Tom chimed in while putting on a sweater due to a wintery cool temperature in his beachside cave home. "Though I must say, Your chivalrous chopping down a Christmas tree to appease Andromeda surprised even me."

"Not cool, Tom. Not cool." Perseus straightened in his chair. "I thought reading minds of Your siblings was something You considered to be a last resort, and not a means of carrying out an innocent chat."

"I did. I still do," Tom retorted, unbothered. "Alan was more than happy to share Your recent escapades with Your guests. One in particular."

"What?" Perseus raised his eyebrow, feeling not only uneasy but unsettled.

"Alan mentioned how much happier You have become since Your guests arrived," Tom continued.

"They are not my guests. They trespassed. They are stuck here because we're snowed in," Perseus puffed out air, unamused.

"Only guilty look for excuses," Luna smiled, surprised that her brothers gazed her way. "What? You guys can take jabs at him, and I can't?"

"No." Perseus brooded.

"I agree with Luna on this one." J.J. smirked, glad the tables appeared to be turning for yet another Alistair brother. "Plus, Your back went up when Tom mentioned Your guests' arrival, but not at the fact he said You were happier since they arrived."

"I'm not happier." Perseus threw his hands up in the air with frustration.

"Sure, I'll buy that one." J.J. chuckled. "But I'm not sure Alan will."

"He doesn't have to." Perseus rose from the chair.

"He won't," Tom grinned while Caelum shook his head.

"I agree with Perseus." Caelum flashed his cocky smile. "It's not like he came up with the story of a damsel in distress and an excuse just to avoid coming down to see us."

"I did not come up with a story of a damsel in distress!" Perseus swore and debated whether to end the call.

"So, she does exist?" Luna asked with a delicate grin.

"Of course, she exists!" Perseus raised his voice. "Didn't Tom and Gunay tell You I had to give her Your linctus vial or she wouldn't have survived because of the poison?!?"

"Alright," Luna raised her hand in surrender.

"Did You figure out the origins of the poison and how it was administered?" Rasalas asked, more intrigued by his brother's reaction than by the idea of Andromeda being poisoned.

"Gunay said something about ricin. I had to rush upstairs to administer Luna's vial when Gunay examined the sample specs I sent over." Perseus moved his shoulders up and down.

"In that case, You better figure out where she got injected with it." Rasalas narrowed his eyebrows, worried.

"She got injected up on the mountain," Perseus replied without thinking.

"Where on her body, brother." Rasalas bit his lip to prevent a chuckle.

"Oh." Perseus stopped pacing around the room.

"Oh." Gunay mocked him, cognizant of Rasalas's train of thought.

"I'd start with her hands. They must have been exposed when that poor excuse of a husband attacked her," Rasalas noted. "That's how I'd do it if I didn't use my culinary skills."

"Huh." J.J. cocked his eyebrow. "Remind me not to eat what You serve."

"Worry not, my man," Rasalas laughed. "Keep my sister and Your kids safe, and I'll keep Your food well done."

"Huh." J.J. repeated, swallowing hard.

"Anyway," Perseus decided to switch the topic, directing his question to Caelum. "Were You able to find out anything more about father's whereabouts in Europe?"

"Nope." Caelum shook his head. "A dead end after a dead end. It's like they meant for us not to find them."

"I honestly hope that was not their main reason for it," Luna frowned.

"I do not think it was." Emmeline nodded while playing with Anya. "When I met Your parents, they seemed like very sincere and loving people."

"Yeah, well, how sincere could they have been about loving their children if they just left us without so much as a note saying they weren't coming back?" Perseus said in one breath, earning a silent gaze of agreement from Tom.

"Would You have allowed them to go out that ominous day if You knew they were heading into evident betrayal?" Emmeline asked, recalling the way she felt when she realized Caelum had been shot and almost lost his life when they faced Amerigo Vincere.

"No." Perseus retorted without hesitation.

"They did what they thought was best for You," J.J. added before Emmeline was able to say anything.

"Well, they could stop hiding since we found out they are still alive," Perseus noted, discontented.

"Maybe the New Year will bring us new leads," Caelum smiled at his twin newborns while overlooking the Mediterranean sea from their patio balcony of Emmeline's grandfather's home. "What do You say kids?"

"Isla and Atlas agree, Papà," Anya smiled at Caelum.

"Are You sure about that?" Caelum grinned at Anya, proud to be able to call her his daughter.

"Sure." Anya nodded with a serious face, only to smile again a moment later.

"Then let us toast to the New Year, and that it will bring us closer to finding mother and father," Luna gushed over the sight of her brother enjoying the bliss of fatherhood.

"I'll drink to that." Perseus saluted them all, and figured he could use a cold glass of whiskey right about now. "Enjoy the New Years, everyone."

"Bye," said those gathered on the other side of the monitors, after which the call transmission ended and Perseus left the underground office, heading upstairs. He swore a silent oath, promising himself to deal with Alan and his blabber mouth of a tongue in the morning. He had to convince his longtime friend he held no feelings for Andromeda. He had no intentions toward her, nor did he go out of his way to show her more than the bare minimum amount of hospitality. And he was almost ready to convince his foolish conscience when he opened the upstairs door to the room, ramming right into Andromeda.

But it wasn't her unexpected presence that ruffled his feathers. Her thoughts did, for they matched his own.

'Oh, my stars...'

≈ **Chapter 13** ≈

For a grown man, owning up to a sudden onset of bashfulness bothered Perseus to the ends of his wit. The fact Alan saw his reaction to Andromeda's appearance right before him as he opened the door to his office room bothered him all the more. And he couldn't find any other way out of the situation except to go through it.

Regardless of how Andromeda's deep and intense gaze made him feel, especially at the small of his neck...

"I did not mean to startle You." She began the conversation due to the obvious lack of response from him aside from a blank stare.

"You didn't." He mumbled after a pause.

"I clearly did." She countered his denial, raising an eyebrow.

"No, You didn't."

"She did." Alan chimed in with a smirk and did not bother to hide it from his best friend.

"I'd stay out of it if I were You." Perseus sent him a look Alan knew all too well, though it had little effect on him - which Perseus noted immediately.

"Who stepped on Your foot?" Alan chuckled.

"You did." Perseus clenched his jaw. "Tom did."

"Ouch." Alan winced, understanding the message Perseus tried to convey.

"Who's Tom?" Andromeda narrowed her eyes on Perseus.

"Nobody." Though Perseus's retort was direct, it did not impress Andromeda.

"Since when would someone like You be bothered if some nobody stepped on Your foot?" She continued without blinking.

"Someone like me?" Perseus looked into her eyes with a piercing gaze. He couldn't tell if her tone of voice or her inconclusive implication bothered him more. "And who am I?"

"Cocky and too full of Yourself," she said matter-of-factly.

"That's my brother." Perseus hissed out before he could stop himself because he thought of Caelum.

"You have a brother?" Andromeda chuckled, thankfully, because the melody that escaped her lips covered Alan's chuckle at the way Perseus just divulged personal information twice now within no more than a minute.

"That's of no concern to You." Perseus grit his teeth because the light shining in Andromeda's eyes disappeared. And he knew he was to blame for it. "I did not mean that."

"Yes, You did." Saying so, Andromeda turned and walked toward Alan sitting at the kitchen table by the window.

"Alan, I did not mean that." Perseus repeated his words.

"I believe our guest had a valid point." Alan sided with Andromeda, earning a gentle smile from her. "You did not need to share the information about Your family. But You did. She did not ask about family - You said it out of Your own conscience. And she should not be blamed for it."

"I did not blame her." Perseus brooded, closing the door to his office behind his back, ensuring it was locked.

"Oh, but You did." Alan nodded.

"Fine." Perseus puffed out air as he approached the table, opting against sitting down. "I apologize for the way I hissed at You."

"Your apology may be warranted, though it is not required. This is Your house," Andromeda linked her hands.

"That may be, but it doesn't mean I should be allowed to speak to You that way," Perseus added, admitting how odd it felt to apologize for defending his privacy.

"Huh." Andromeda raised her eyebrow, rising from the chair to stand face to face with him. "If You feel that way, then I accept Your apology on Your terms."

"What does that mean?" Perseus tipped his head back, confused.

"It means what I meant for it to mean." She smiled and extended her hand in a sign of truce. "You figure it out."

"Do You always argue this way?" Perseus asked, accepting her hand in a handshake.

"This? This was not an argument," she smiled wider. "I know when I'm on losing ground. I just adapt quicker than some people."

"Do You?" Perseus looked down at their joined hands, then looked up at her. "Mind if we step outside? I need to speak with You about something."

"Not at all," she shook her head and turned to Alan. "Would You mind looking after my sons?"

"They are fine grown men. They do not need me looking after them. I thought I could join You outside," Alan wondered, teasing Perseus to see his reaction, which Perseus figured out without a problem.

"No. You've caused enough mischief," Perseus protested.

"What did I do?" Alan asked innocently.

"Ask Tom." Perseus shot him another direct gaze.

"Ouch." Alan raised his hands.

"You got that right." This time Perseus shot him a grin, which disappeared as quickly as it appeared. He walked over to the coats hanging by the door, grabbing two of them. "I need to speak with Andromeda alone. We will be right back."

"Why does it sound so negative?" Andromeda inquired, hesitant.

"Because it is." Perseus retorted flatly.

"Oh," she whispered.

"Not that negative." Perseus attempted to smile, which resulted in an insincere smirk that had the opposite effect on Andromeda. He grabbed one of the thick highlander handwoven wool blankets and opened the door for her.

"I guess I do not have much choice." Andromeda looked at Alan and zipped up her jacket.

"I guess not." Alan moved his shoulders, smiling to himself as Perseus placed the blanket on Andromeda's shoulders, secured it tighter around her, and closed the door behind them...

Chapter 14

The crisp mountain air caressing Perseus's cheek affected his grumpy mood the moment he closed the door behind him after stepping outside onto the front porch with Andromeda. So much so, that it... disappeared at once, causing his worry lines to smooth out. There was something indescribably calming in the way the evening mountain breeze, mixed with the gentle warm rays of the sun, made him feel. Even in the winter. Even on New Year's Eve. Especially on New Year's Eve.

He smiled. He could not help it. Nor would he have tried. There were many reasons why he chose to settle in the little cottage hidden far from civilization in the Ku Dziurze Gorge near the Ku Dziurze stream. Was it because Alan saved his life not far from where the cottage stood and suggested he moved in? Perhaps. Was it because Perseus felt that his loneliness did not feel so lonely if he didn't compare his life to others daily since he did not have to see happy couples or fulfilled happy families going about their happy daily routines? Possibly. Was it because being so far from human development brought him closer to nature and the night sky he so very much loved deep in his heart? That question required no answer - it was as evident to him as it became evident to Andromeda.

"I thought You were going to scold me into the next century, but..." Andromeda began to speak yet cut her words short the moment he looked at her. His deeply content gaze derailed her train of thought, and she could have sworn his eyes softened in the evening sun. She forgot her words. She forgot his brooding mood from a minute ago. She forgot his irritable self-righteous cockiness.

"But?" Perseus raised his eyebrow, zipping his jacket all the way up. He was used to the cold mountain breezes, and he respected its virtues. Staying warm was one of its requisites.

"But what?" Andromeda asked, not having blinked in a while. She just stared - either at him or at her own awkwardness, and she could not help it. So, he helped her - by smiling with such sincerity it caused her to shake her head.

"But what? You are the one who said You thought I would scold You then cut Your words mid-sentence." He continued to smile, unaware he hadn't smiled this sincerely in a conversation with someone aside from his family or Alan for years.

"Oh." She replied, feeling self-conscious. "Well, umm. It's just odd that Your face changed the moment You stepped outside into the sun."

"My face is odd?" Perseus raised his other eyebrow.

"No!" She turned to him, shocked at the accusation. "That is not what I meant!"

"Nor did You mean to startle me back there, inside, but You did, and here we are," he chuckled, making her feel even more self-conscious.

"Right. Sorry, but I really did not mean to startle You."

"An apology followed by an excuse devoids sincerity from Your intentions."

"Those are some wise words, even for You."

"Ouch."

"I didn't mean..."

"Oh, but You did." He felt a pang of something unfamiliar and somehow gratifying in his gut at the gesture, and he could not figure out why. So, he moved closer to the porch's wooden hand-carved railing.

"Fine." She walked toward the railing, but on the opposite side of the door, deciding to put distance between them. "You have a beautiful home. With a beautiful view."

"Thanks." He replied without looking at her. He looked outward, at the grounds in front of his house, at the trees surrounding the property, at the Ku Dziurze stream so close to the front porch he could hear the drops of water hitting the snowy banks and rocks exposed above the surface of the stream, at the grand mountains rising to high heavens from behind the trees. "It's my own kind of paradise."

"It feels that way, too." She agreed with his words. "I have lived in many places, but nothing compares to the mountains."

"Did You really?" He wondered, intrigued. "Do You travel a lot? I mean, did You before...?"

"Before the man I promised to cherish for as long as I lived decided to put an expiration date on that?" She shook her head, wrapping the blanket tighter around her. "No, I would not call it travel."

"What would You call it then?"

"Escaping the pain of the past." She closed her eyes, turning her face to the setting sun.

"You don't strike me as a fragile type afraid of her past."

"And You don't strike me as someone caring about strangers. I did not say I was afraid of my past. I said I lived in many places to escape the pain."

"Isn't that the same?"

"No. Haven't You ever lived through a painful experience where the pain of it lingers in Your heart until today, but You hold no fear over it?"

"That... is true," he agreed, recalling the loss of his parents so many years ago.

"I lost my family in a house explosion." She whispered, looking down on her hands resting on the snow-covered railing. She felt the cold of the snow, yet it paled in comparison with the numbing void in her soul. "One minute everyone was alive, the next I was gasping for air at the realization I would never see them again."

'I know how it feels...'

Glad he whispered those excruciating words in his mind, Perseus fisted his hands in the pockets of his coat. "How old were You?"

"No older than Tristan. The kitchen gas tank exploded when I went to the shed to get more firewood for the living room fireplace." The memories no longer hurt, but the guilt so very much did.

"It must have been tough to go through," he stepped closer without realizing he had done so.

"It was." She looked up at him briefly, then gazed back down on her hands. "But what hurts the most is the guilt. I still carry it to this day."

"Why would You feel guilty? If You had stayed in the house, we may not have been having this conversation," he said with sincerity, suddenly struck by the memories from the day the Alistair siblings found out about their parents' passing.

"True. But the guilt doesn't come from surviving while they had not. It comes from knowing I fought with my dad about going out into the cold to get more of that stupid wood."

"You didn't know leaving to get the wood would save Your life," he noted, feeling a sudden connection with her.

"Nor did I know that the last memory I would ever have of my family would be of us arguing about some mundane chore of fetching wood." She turned to him, not finding it surprising that he stood right beside her now. She found it rather comforting.

"Or realizing that the mundane chore ended up saving Your life..." he whispered because his throat locked up.

"How did Your parents die?" Though the question Andromeda posed was innocent, and one with which she hoped to strike a connection with him, she could not have foreseen Perseus's reaction.

"How the hell do You know about my parents?!?" His raised voice caused her shoulders to bend inwards. It wasn't the volume that frightened her, it was the ice-cold tone filled with accusation.

"I don't know anything about Your parents. I simply asked because You seemed to understand how I felt." She straightened and turned to head back inside, but he reached for her, placing a hand on her shoulder.

"I... did not mean to shout at You."

"But You did. Deal with it. We are not friends. Nor are we acquaintances forced to keep in touch once we leave Your house. I will tell my sons our stay here has come to an end."

"Stop it." He stood in her way now. "You cannot leave. Not yet."

"And why yet?" She tipped her chin up. "We are obviously not welcome here. I lived through enough to see that. We will leave tomorrow."

"No, You won't." He took a step forward.

"I do not need Your permission to leave. Nor do I need Your help."

"Yes, You do."

"And why would that be?" She tipped her chin up higher.

He leaned in, ensuring no one inside the house could hear him, coming dangerously close to her lips, and whispered looking into her eyes. "Because I still need to remove the poison still left in You..."

Chapter 15

He knew it. He just knew it. Too bad he realized it a heartbeat too late. The words that spilled from his lips, warning Andromeda of traces of poison still left in her body, were meant to convince her she could not leave his mountain cottage just yet. They were not meant to backfire right in his face. Or his gut.

The fear that washed over Andromeda struck him so suddenly he could not dismiss it. The fear for her life. The fear for the lives of her sons. The fear of the possibility of them going through life without her in it. It all rang loud in her thoughts, so easily read by him. And it all showed in her eyes. Eyes looking up at him with the rays of the setting sun shining ever so delicately over her face.

He leaned in to whisper the words into her ear. It was as innocent as his intention was. Yet what he thought when he realized he could not look away from her frightened piercing gaze felt anything but innocent.

"Will I die?" She whispered, frightened more than she would like to have revealed.

"Not if I can help it."

"I doubt that."

"I know what to do."

"You also know no boundaries when it comes to making someone feel unwelcome." She turned to go back inside, but he followed her lead, blocking her path again. "Maybe I have traces of the poison still left in my system, maybe not. I survived this long because I counted on myself. I do not need to count on some self-centered Mountain Man macho with a misplaced hero syndrome."

"What?" He chuckled. His siblings called him many things, but never that. "You think I have a misplaced hero syndrome?"

"That's evident." She scoffed. Since stepping to the side would not have worked.

"Not to me." He crossed his arms at his chest. "I may help people in need, but that is not because I need validation for some misplaced sense of righteousness."

"How about looking for rectification for whatever You think You did wrong in the past?" She took a jab at his conscience. And, oh! Was it a direct hit to the bullseye! Even if he didn't show it.

"You don't know me."

"I would say the same thing about You. I've dealt with my share of vain men in my life. I can recognize one when I see one."

"Well, You sure picked the right one for Your husband." His temper may have flared, but the moment he said those words, albeit absent-mindedly, Andromeda took such a decisive step toward him he took one back. It was not cowardice on his part, he thought. It was a... precautionary measure.

"What do You know about my husband?!?" She whispered in a way she may as well been shouting. Not because of the harshness of the words, but because of the slew of emotions rushing through her thoughts.

Aware he had crossed the line he would have to cross at some point if Andromeda and her sons were to stay at his cottage any longer, Perseus sighed a heavy sigh and decided to reveal to her what he knew. "I know he's dead."

"What?"

"And from what I gather, I'd say Tristan pushed the man to his death to save You."

"What?" She repeated, covering her mouth. "How... how do You know?"

"I was called to search for You. I was still down the mountain when a man fell from a considerable height to his death."

"Are You sure he died?"

"Well, it looked like his lifeline turned pretty flat to me."

"That is an awful thing to say."

"Not as awful as trying to kill Your own wife and the mother of Your children."

"How... how did You know he was my husband? Did You recognize him?"

"Well, facial recognition was out of the question the way he splattered face-first." Perseus grimaced with a bit of amusement, adjusting his grin when she sent him a judging look. "No. I did not recognize him. I figured he was the boys' father because I heard one of them when I looked up to see where the man could have fallen from."

"How could You have heard them? We were really high up when Stoyan caught up with us."

"I'm a... good listener," he cleared his throat. "Stoyan? Does not ring a bell."

"Nor should it since You are a good man."

"I thought I was a self-centered Mountain Man macho with a misplaced hero syndrome?"

"You can be both."

"Agree to agree." He chuckled. "So, Stoyan, huh? Sounds like a lowlife to me."

"I wish someone could have told me that the day I met him," she nudged him, with a grimace.

"That bad?" He wondered, already anticipating the answer, and hoped she would reveal the man's full name. She did.

"Stoyan Natan was a charming honorable gentleman when I met him. He caught my attention because he was very protective of his young son when I met him in Vienna." Running a hand through her hair, she adjusted the blanket. Not because of the evening breeze, but because of the memories.

"Young son?" Perseus sent her a puzzling look. "Is Tristan not Your son?"

"He is. In every way possible aside from the biological one," she smiled. "It took one look into Tristan's sad eyes, and I knew I would have done everything in my power to bring joy back to his life."

"Why?" He asked more out of curiosity than out of empathy.

"After my family passed away, I felt alone. All alone. No one cared for me, no one cared about me. I moved from town to town, backpacked from country to country through the mountains or deserted passages. I paid my way through by working hard, never leaving any debt or trace of my name behind. Meeting Stoyan and Tristan made me feel as if I was needed." She closed her eyes, fighting a battle with tears. "Stoyan clouded my mind with the idea of love, of finding someone he and his son could finally belong to."

"Sounds pretty convincing."

"It sure did. And I thought that for a longer while," she scoffed with self-pity. "But after Liam and Kai were born Stoyan made it clear to me that I was the one who belonged to him."

"Is that why You ran?" He asked. Somehow it no longer felt like simple curiosity. The Alistair blood in him simmered with a temper due to his sense of righteousness.

"No. That was long ago. My sons needed a father, even though Stoyan no longer needed me to believe he loved me. Picture-perfect families can hide unhappiness in exceptionally convincing ways."

"So, what changed?" Perseus leaned in, opting to shove his fisted hands into the pockets of his washed-out jeans instead of allowing Andromeda to see his reaction.

"I overheard him telling someone that I influenced his sons too much, especially Tristan. His sons may have needed a mother, but they should have become tougher - like him." She looked inside through the kitchen window, and smiled, seeing Liam and Kai sitting around the Christmas tree. She smiled wider when Tristan walked into the room and stood near Alan.

She turned back, looking at Perseus with eyes he knew then and there he would never be able to forget. "I cannot fathom what type of a tyrant would consider dismissing his own children because they didn't fit his definition of a stern businessman."

'I'm glad Tristan shoved him to save You...'

"What did You say?" Andromeda shot him a blunt stare. One he could not dismiss...

Chapter 16

"Damn..."

It took less than half of a split second for the chilling wave of sheer fear to travel from Perseus's gut through his heart all the way up to his mind. Standing on the porch of his mountain cottage, in the one place on earth that always felt like a safe haven, Perseus felt as if his knees were about to buckle under the weight of his inexplicably heavy... regret.

Did he really do that? Did he just save the life of a stranger with the innocent use of a linctus vial containing his sister's DNA - the ALISTAIR DNA - and by doing so enabled the woman standing before him to acquire their family trait of reading minds. Did he?!?

He swallowed hard. Blinked. Nay, he blinked twice. And stood so still Andromeda began to wonder about his well-being.

"Are You alright?" Andromeda reached for him, but he took a step back.

"I will be right back. Don't move." He warned her, pointing at her as he turned toward the door. "DON'T MOVE."

"Why?" She narrowed her eyebrows, but Perseus did not get a chance to see the puzzled look on her face. Nor did he notice the surprised faces of three boys gathered in the kitchen by the Christmas tree. Nor did he even acknowledge Alan's presence in the office room as he shut the door behind him after walking into the office. He turned the lock on the doorknob, turned around to head toward the fireplace, and all but fell backwards against the door as Alan stepped right in front of him.

"Damn!" Perseus jolted from the shock of seeing his best friend so unexpectedly.

"Yeah, double that." Alan narrowed his eyes at Perseus's stunned reaction. "You spend two minutes alone with a woman and Your senses freak out?"

"Shut up." Perseus hissed out, making his way toward the fireplace. "You'd freak out, too."

"She's a wonderful woman." Alan continued to grin. "How on earth could she have caused You to react like this? Did You tell her You liked her and she said she did not find mountain men like You attractive?"

"No." Perseus stopped, dismayed, and shot Alan an irritated look. "No! It's much worse than that!"

"She said she *did* find You attractive?" Alan mocked him, even more amused.

"Alan, please!" Perseus walked back to Alan and leaned in, whispering. "She read my mind."

"Your mind isn't exactly hard to read when Your temper fumes out of Your ears," Alan dismissed the notion.

"I won't respond to that." Perseus straightened up. "Alan, she READ my mind."

"Are You sure?"

"Yes. No." Perseus shook his head, frustrated. "Yes."

"Which one is it?"

"I don't know." Perseus muttered. "I need to speak with Luna."

"What can she do?" Alan tipped his head to the side. "Don't You think Tom could help more in this case?"

"No." Perseus opened the hidden door in the fireplace. "He'd have a fit. I need to be sure about this before I speak to him."

"Do You think there could be any possibility she hid the fact she could read minds as well?" Alan's eyes grew wide. "What if she's just like You? What if her sons can read minds, too?"

"What are the chances of that?" Perseus grit his teeth with anger at himself, pointing at the door. "What if it was a result of me administering Luna's damn vial?"

"Maybe." Alan scratched his head. "Did Caelum ever verify if Anya could read minds?"

"That kid was a whiz before I administered the vial to her. I doubt she'll reveal if she knows how to read minds anytime soon even if she does," Perseus explained as both men made their way down to Perseus's underground office filled with high tech equipment.

"Well, Aurora did begin to read minds, didn't she?" Alan continued with the questions while Perseus turned on the monitor linked to Luna's monitor back in Boston.

"She sure did. But that was because of the blood transfusion. Not because of a vial with an insignificant trace of Luna's blood/"

"It is not insignificant if it carries within it the healing power to save a life. Do You think Luna will be able to help You?"

"I hope so. I need to be certain before we tell Tom. He's going to be furious if this is true." Saying so, Perseus sat down behind the desk and began typing on the lit-up keyboard. "Let's hope Luna confirms there is no way my suspicion could be true."

"I thought Tom was aware You were going to use the linctus vial on Andromeda?"

"Yeah, well, that was before we had any idea the vial could do more than save lives," Perseus rubbed his beard once more as Luna's smiling face appeared on the monitor screen.

"Missed me already?" Luna greeted them, waving a hand in a sincere gesture when she noticed Alan standing beside her brother.

"Definitely, my dear." Alan waved back. "But I am afraid our call is of a different nature."

"Oh?" Luna's smile disappeared. "What's wrong?"

"Andromeda read my mind." The urgency in Perseus's voice matched the fear in his eyes. Alan did not notice it, but Luna did not need to read her brother's thoughts to figure out what was going through his mind.

"She did?" Luna whispered, taken aback by the news. "How's that possible?"

"Well, actually, we were hoping You could tell us there isn't any possibility of this being true." Alan inquired before Perseus could shake off the ill feeling twisting knots in his gut.

"Why me?" Luna sat down behind the desk in her office, confused.

"Because I think I screwed up by saving Andromeda's life when I administered Your vial to her."

"You screwed up by saving her life?" Luna asked, stunned.

"No!" Perseus raised his voice.

"Then I do not see how You could be upset with Yourself," Luna tipped her head to the side.

"Did You miss the part where I mentioned I think Andromeda read my mind?!?" Perseus puffed out air.

"First of all, how do You know she did read Your mind?" Luna leaned forward.

"I thought about Tristan pushing Andromeda's husband to save their lives..."

"Who's Tristan?" Luna wondered.

"Andromeda's son. He is the one who pushed his father down the mountain," Alan chimed in.

"He has a handsome name," Luna patted her pregnant belly. "Mind if I consider it for our bundle of joy?"

"Yes. Do concentrate on the matter at hand, sister." Perseus grit his teeth. "I thought of him, and she must have read my mind."

"And?" Luna leaned in a bit more.

"And...? She asked if I said something." The recollection of that moment replayed itself in his mind. And it felt even worse this time around.

"That's it?" Luna chuckled.

"Isn't that enough?" Perseus replied assertively.

"No. Imagine You told Tom about it, and it turned out not to be true," she rolled her eyes. "He'd mock You for it into eternity."

"She's right." Alan agreed.

"She is?" Perseus lowered his shoulders in a sign of surrender.

"I am." Luna nodded, not entirely convinced, though she blocked her mind off to Perseus for the moment. "Do us all a favor and test her to see if she really can or cannot read Your mind."

"How do I do that?" Perseus asked, suddenly dumbfounded.

"Think of kissing her and see what she does," Luna wiggled her eyebrows, teasing her brother.

"Are You insane?!?" Perseus rose from the chair. "She just lost her husband!"

"Relax, Mountain Boy." Luna giggled while Alan bit his lip to prevent a smirk. "Besides, tell me why the idea of her husband just dying bothers You more than the idea of kissing her?"

"Luna!" Perseus scolded her.

"Why are You mad at Your sister?" J.J. Monroe joined his wife, worried that Perseus raised his voice.

"Because she's impossible!" Perseus retorted with a temper.

"Why?" J.J. embraced Luna.

"Because I told him to think of kissing Andromeda," Luna smirked at J.J. with unmistakable mischief.

"Double damn!" J.J. raised his hand in a high-five gesture. "Mountain Boy, way to ring in the new year!"

"Shut up," Perseus leaned in toward the monitor. "Why did I even bother calling You?"

"To calm Your conscience." Alan explained, earning a leveled look from Perseus.

"What he said." Luna sent a wide smile Alan's way.

"Whatever." Perseus shook his head. "You want to help clear my conscience? See if You can dig up anything on Stoyan Natan."

"Who?" J.J. inquired with suspicion.

"Andromeda's ex-husband." Perseus clenched his jaw.

"Glad he's out of the picture if You're considering puckering up to her." J.J. noted, raising his hands in defense. "What? I meant it for good. For Andromeda's good."

"He's right." Luna patted her husband's hand. "From what You described; she must have gone through a lot with that man."

"She did." Perseus sighed. "Alright. Enough chit-chatting. I have to speak with Andromeda."

"You do that." J.J. flashed his pearly whites. "Do let us know how the kissing went."

"Monroe!" Perseus exclaimed.

"Happy New Year, Mountain Boy." J.J. winked at Perseus and waved casually at Alan. "Happy New Year, Alan."

"You too, Sir." Alan grinned. "Don't worry, I'll make sure Perseus behaves."

"Oh, I bet on it." J.J. winked at Alan, right before Perseus turned the monitor off. Though the sight of Luna and J.J. Monroe disappeared, J.J.'s mischievous laugh echoed through the room, bouncing off the walls carved out in mountain rock.

"Not a word." Perseus pointed at Alan.

"Wouldn't dream of it." Alan raised his hands. "But You might want to rush upstairs. There is someone waiting for You on the porch, and I gauge the sun already went down behind the mountain peaks.

"Damn," was all Perseus whispered as he rushed upstairs, then once more, surprised to find no trace of Andromeda on the porch...

≈ Chapter 17 ≈

To acknowledge the fact he was searching the premises of his homestead for the woman who raised his temper by a hundred degrees validated to Perseus that he... wanted to find her. Which meant that he began to slowly comprehend the gravity of her presence. Much to his own discomfort.

Making his way around the cottage, with the undisturbed sound of snow creaking under his feet, Perseus breathed heavily as he looked for any sign of Andromeda. Finding none, he decided to head back inside. The dark night sky did little to aid in his search. Scarce stars, so out of the ordinary for this time of the year, did not help either. And the moon, usually shining above his cottage, hid on the other side of the mountains.

Resigned, Perseus swore under his breath, skimmed the area in front of the cottage one last time, and stepped onto the porch. It was then that he caught a glimpse of a dark shadowy figure standing by the trees along the edge of the Ku Dziurze stream, dangerously close to the cloaked wall protecting the premises.

'Andromeda...'

The thought that formed in his mind both calmed and unnerved him. He should not have been this pleased to find her. He should not have been this glad to realize she waited outside for him. He should not have been this eager to make his way to where she stood. And yet... he was.

"I thought I told You not to move." He scolded Andromeda, deciding to cover up his relieved reaction with one she would have anticipated.

"You may have told me not to move. But You took Your time, so I grew tired of waiting and decided to wait for You out here instead. I'd call it a compromise."

"Yeah." Perseus grit his teeth. "You could have compromised Your safety, is what You could have done."

"I doubt anyone would be foolish enough to make their way all the way up here," she grinned in the dimmed light.

"I thought the same thing a week ago. And yet, I'm looking at You now."

"Wise guy, aren't You?" Andromeda laughed and turned back to look at the stream flowing freely mere feet away from them. "Alan said there's a good side to You underneath that macho façade."

"Again with the macho reference?" He raised a brow. "Why do You insist on comparing me to someone like that?"

"You're a perfect example of it." She clicked her tongue, causing him to crack up. "Would You prefer if I called You a brooding Mountain Man?"

"Why brooding?" He asked, in an obvious brooding tone.

"I believe You just answered Your own question." She smirked, breathing in the calm night air. "I've said it before, I will say it again. You have a beautiful place here. The nature. The serenity. The peace of it all."

"I see no reason to disagree with You."

"That would be a first."

"Am I really that awful of a host?"

"You don't compare to Alan. You're in a class of Your own."

"Ouch."

"Though, I must say, I will be forever grateful to You for tending to my sons in the past week." She turned to him. "Not everyone would do that."

"Alan did most of the tending." Perseus moved his shoulders, somehow uncomfortable accepting the compliment.

"Alan did not surprise the boys with a personally chopped down Christmas tree, nor presents under it."

"They weren't opulent presents." He dismissed the notion he did anything out of the ordinary or intentional.

"Not everyone goes for opulent gifts. Some would give everything for a sincere gift, even the smallest in size. Believe me."

"Would You?"

"Yes." She looked up at the branches and peaks of the pine trees on the other side of the stream swaying gently in the mountain wind under the weight of the heavy freshly fallen wet snow. "It's been a long time since I received something of value to my heart that hadn't come from my sons."

"Hadn't Your dearly deceased husband bestowed opulent gifts on You?" Perseus asked, biting his tongue for poor timing of the question. "Sorry."

"Your question did not call for an apology." She looked down, eventually gazing up at him with the kind of sad eyes that pulled at his gut. "Stoyan was a wealthy man. Yet he knew little about the true meaning of a family. Some throw gold and diamonds at their families, blindly unaware that one sincere embrace would be enough for a child yearning for a father's affection."

"And what would be enough for a wife?" He bit his tongue for a second time, stupefied why he kept asking her such private questions.

"Not extravagant gifts. That would be for sure," she said quietly. "I have yearned for a deeper connection with someone ever since losing my family. I fell for Stoyan's words and didn't see his true nature until it was too late."

"You are not the only one to have done so," he whispered, thinking of Rasalas and the way Tom and Luna had to come to his rescue.

"If You could wish upon a starry night, such as tonight, what would You wish for?" He wondered and gazed up at the sky above them. The night grew dark, and the fact they were miles away from all other properties and homes added to the privacy of the location.

"I wish I could have had the ability to read minds back then," she noted so matter-of-factly it raised the hair at the small of his neck.

"WHAT?!?" He exclaimed, creating an echoing boom through the Ku Dziurze Gorge and the mountain range, causing her shoulders to arch inwards.

"Why are You yelling?"

"Why did You say You wanted to read minds?" He asked in a quieter tone, though still loud enough to sound off in an echo.

"Doesn't everybody wish for that?" She offered him a level look. "But if I would have seen through him back then, I never would have met Liam or Kai. That alone was worth it."

"That... is an oddly logical point of view," he rubbed at his beard. "I guess life has a way of making sense in retrospect."

"Yeah," she sighed. "Too bad it cannot be lived backwards. Then we could prepare for the heartache and disappointments."

"Yeah." He decided to switch topics. "About that wish? Aside from wishing for the ability to read minds, what else would You wish for?"

"I'd wish for a flower."

"A flower?" He raised his eyebrows, surprised. "In the middle of winter?"

"Yes. You asked what I would wish for. Why are You judging me for being honest again?"

"Sorry." He apologized, feeling tactless. "Why a flower?"

"Because I've received countless flowers in the past, yet not one of them was ever given to me with sincerity."

"What flower would You wish for?"

"A Blue Hollyhock," she smiled, scaring him in the most profound way.

"You cannot be serious."

"First You judge my choice of a wish, then ridicule me for it?" She tipped her chin up, turning around to head back to the cottage. "I can't figure You out, and I don't think I should try. All I know is that You are rude beyond limits."

"I did not mean to offend You." He reached for her, holding onto her hand. "I reacted the way I did because Blue Hollyhocks are my favorite flowers."

"You have a favorite flower?"

"How come You can judge me?"

"Like I'm the only one between us who's judgmental?" She retorted sarcastically. "Please, may I have my hand back?"

"No."

"No?" She turned back toward him. "And why not?"

"Because I think I figured out where the ricin pellet that poisoned You was injected," was all he whispered, realizing he accomplished his goal of getting her attention.

"Are You... certain?" She stepped closer toward him and did not protest when he raised their joined hands higher, toward the moonlight which finally shone above them.

"I think so." He brought her hand closer to his eyes to examine it, gently rubbing his thumb over a barely noticeable tiny bump under her skin on the left wrist. "We should remove it. The antidote neutralized the poison for now, but leaving the pellet where it is could still harm You."

"We?" She opened her eyes wide.

"If You prefer to do it Yourself, be my guest. But You must know I'm a professional," he explained, unaware he was still gently rubbing at her wrist with his thumb.

"You're a perfectionist not a professional."

"One can be both."

"I doubt that in Your case," she smirked insincerely.

"Keep judging me, and I'll find a way to prove it to You." He leaned in, whispering the words with such intensity she did not even feel the swift and proficient tiny cut on her wrist as the ricin pellet was pulled out from underneath her skin. The only thing she felt was the inexplicably undeniable tug on her heart...

Chapter 18

He held her hand. What harm could it have done? None, whatsoever. He believed it. He *wanted* to believe it. There was nothing wrong with tending to the wounded person who he just so happened to save for the second time from the injected poison.

And yet...

What started as an innocent gesture of holding Andromeda's hand somehow morphed into holding onto it. In a not-so-innocent way.

As Andromeda's gaze softened, so did his. Was it the serenity of the night? Was it the cool mountain breeze turning into an icy caress of their cheeks? Was it the moonlight which finally deemed appropriate - or rather, mischievously opportune - to shine its full glow on two unexpecting souls searching for something they did not know was within their grasp?

If only they let down their defenses...

"Why did You do that?" Andromeda's curious whisper reached Perseus's ears as if held within it the key to bringing him back into the realm of reality he did not know he had lost touch with.

"What?" He blinked, a bit disoriented, immediately releasing her hand. "I did not hold Your hand because of any ulterior motives. I had a reason for it."

"I bet."

Her sudden and subtle smile struck him as odd, especially because of how coldly she acted toward him a moment ago. So, he did what he knew best. He decided to flip the conversation on her once more. "Why are You smiling?"

"Because it's not a crime." She narrowed her eyes. "Isn't surviving a potentially lethal poison something to smile about?"

"I guess." He felt dumb. Why shouldn't she have been able to smile? Why? Did she need his permission? No. The mere thought of it caused him to shove hands in the pockets of his jacket. It was not cowardice. It was... his usual gesture of acknowledging his opponent's better judgment. "You should know I took hold of Your hand to remove the poisonous pellet from Your wrist. It's gone now."

"And You denied having a hero complex."

"I don't have a..." he cut his words short because of what he saw in her eyes, and it somehow struck him as... comforting. So comforting, in fact, it brought on a wave of uneasiness. Uneasiness that overshadowed his desire to figure out if Andromeda did in fact end up possessing the ability to read minds. "We should head back inside. It's pretty chilly out here."

"I'll say." She adjusted the blanket around her shoulders, aware of his reaction which had nothing to do with the chilly mountain air. "Don't worry, Perseus. I am not interested in any sort of connection with You. Men like You are not my type. Besides, we'll be gone and out of Your life in a couple of days."

"Why would I worry?" He attempted to brush her retort off, though her directness caused him to feel insulted, despite the facade of being unaffected by her words.

"Whatever happened to You in the past has You running scared when it comes to closer interactions with people." She tipped her head, turning toward the house, with her back against the stream. "I find it amusing, and childish to be more precise."

"I'm not childish."

"No?" She countered. "I was forced to go through life counting on only myself. My husband was a tyrant. I would be the first to admit it. But I would also be first to admit I need my sons to survive because one cannot go through life relying only on loneliness."

"I am not lonely." He took a step forward, telling himself the temper she stirred in him had nothing to do with the bottled-up feelings he had kept at bay for too many years.

"Fine, then." She nodded. "You are not a man with a misplaced hero complex, nor a childish man, nor someone who is lonely. But You sure aren't confident enough to defend who You are or what You feel."

"What I feel?" He chuckled so sarcastically it came off as a cowardly response. "What is it that You think I feel since You have read me so well in the few days since You trespassed onto my property?"

"I did not trespass onto Your property. I wasn't conscious when my sons decided to seek shelter here," she tipped her head up confidently. "As for You? I may have had a lonely marriage the last few years, but it is You who chooses loneliness, even in the company of those who have no choice but to spend time with You."

"You are correct. You are definitely full of Yourself but correct, nonetheless." He took another step forward and noticed that her flared-up temper... lowered his. He looked into her eyes and felt nonchalant because of her reaction. "I chose loneliness. I chose it long ago. But my loneliness has nothing to do with feeling lonely. It was my choice. Just as Yours was to stay with someone who failed to see the value of Your life and lives of his sons."

"Feeling better? That's probably the first sincere statement I heard from You since we met."

"I am sincere in everything I say and do."

"I bet." She shook her head. "You're just not sincere with Yourself."

"You have no right to say that about me."

"Perhaps." Andromeda moved her shoulders, unimpressed by his abrupt display of masculinity. "But I am a grown woman, and I am capable of making up my mind about those I come across on my path."

"Oh, and what? Escaping from Your husband made You an expert on human behavior?" He hissed out, cognizant of what his underhanded punch line meant only after he said it.

"No." She retorted with barely noticeable tears. "Being hurt by life itself too many times made me one."

"I..." his throat locked up from guilt.

"Save it." She raised her hand. "I appreciate Your help. I really do. I also appreciate the fact You didn't take advantage of the situation. At least You are man enough for that."

"What advantage are You referring to?" He tipped his head, taken aback by her directness.

"I'm talking about making a pass at me or trying to see if I would allow anything more than Your landlord-like treatment."

"That is a bold statement for someone who just lost her husband." His eyes widened. He may have possessed the ability to read minds, and there have been times where he chose not to read others' thoughts, but he seldom felt astonished by someone's bluntness. Andromeda not only astonished him, but somehow found a way to insult his masculinity - yet again.

"A husband whose top priority was to put an end to my existence," she said coldly. "I swore to myself a while back that I would make it my priority to put myself first. That also includes my feelings."

"And yet You judged me for choosing myself first. Not at all hypocritical, right?"

"We're done here." She turned to make her way back to the house, slipping on the uneven snow-covered rocky ground by the Ku Dziurze stream. Much to her horror, she reached for him to save herself from the fall. To make matters worse, he lost his footing as well because of the icy banks of the stream, falling backwards - and by doing so pulled her with him. They tumbled.

He swore. She yelped. And both landed in the most unforgiving manner, lips touching even if they tried to pretend it wasn't so...

≈ Chapter 19 ≈

His mind went blank. Completely, utterly, and deliriously blank. For the first time in his life because of a woman...

Andromeda tripped. True. But he lost his footing just the same. Through no fault of their own - or so he tried to convince himself of it.

The fact of the matter was, she was going to fall. They both knew it. And she reached for him in a last attempt to prevent the inevitable fall they feared was coming. He reached for her as well. He was certain he was steady enough on his feet to save her. But nature governed itself with its own laws, and in some cases, gravity won over human intentions. Especially against overly confident brute mountain men.

They were now stuck. In every sense of the word. Perseus was stuck, laying underneath Andromeda, with his back half-submerged in the rocky bottom and icy waters of the Ku Dziurze stream. Andromeda was stuck, laying atop Perseus, half-stricken by guilt and half-awestruck by the waves of emotions rushing through her because of a kiss as they tumbled to the ground.

And neither of them seemed to know what to do next...

'Who on earth kisses like that...!?!'

"I beg Your pardon?" He whispered against her lips, shocked by her astonishment regarding the kiss.

"Well, You should!" She tipped her head back, hoping to high heavens he would accept the blame for their fall - which she knew perfectly well was a result of her own clumsiness. He knew so as well. "This is Your fault!"

"You might say that." He grinned, not referring to the fall.

"Why on earth are You smiling?" She asked, taken aback by his stoic gaze illuminated by moonlight causing his eyes to appear more mischievous.

"Double damn, I'm not sure." His smile widened. "Maybe because I did not expect for this to happen."

"No?" She puffed out air. "I wouldn't be so sure."

"I would."

"I told You that You're not my type," she tried to adjust her position, failing because of his strong grip.

"So, You said." He agreed, paying little attention to the freezing surface of the stream underneath him. "I had no intention of causing this fall."

"And You had no intention of kissing me either, right?" She grit her teeth, realizing that they laid on the banks of the stream.

"No."

"That is a lie."

"Oh?" He raised his eyebrow. "You're calling me a liar?"

"You're telling me You did not think of kissing me?"

"That's not the same." Perseus flashed his pearly whites, and she could see the amusement in his eyes. "Curiosity is far from taking action, especially in this case."

"What does that even mean?"

"You're not my type," he said so matter-of-factly her temper flared.

'Why not...?'

The thought both amused him and somehow delighted him on a level he found intriguing. "I have a rule of not getting involved with those I rescue."

"You did not rescue me." She blurted out, somehow upset.

"Maybe not out there..." he glanced up toward the mountains towering above and around them. "But I did save Your life - twice now. Maybe even three times."

"Three?" She protested, failing once more to rise on her elbows. Perseus's grip may have turned from strong to less intense, but there was nothing weak in the way he held her.

"Once from the poison - in my bed. Second time from the pellet stuck under the skin in Your wrist. And now a third time when You fell on top of me." Oh, he felt good. Better than good! Kissing Andromeda may have been purely unintentional and coincidental, but it made him feel good about the turn of events. He felt even better now.

"I was right." She scoffed.

"About what?"

"You ARE a self-centered Mountain Man macho with a misplaced hero syndrome."

"Maybe." An impulse rushed through him to kiss her again. Once more, even if only once more because he knew nothing good would come of it.

"Perseus?" She grew worried, lowering her gaze.

"Yes?" He tightened his grip.

"Are You sure I will be alright?" The worry in her eyes sounded even more daunting in her voice.

"Yes," he replied with confidence. "Why? Do You still feel the effect of the poison? That will pass."

"I am not sure what I feel," she shook her head, searching for the right words. "Are there any side effects from the poison that may be permanent?"

"Like what?"

"Like... hearing voices?" She asked, feeling foolish.

"Hearing voices?" He paled, even in the moonlight.

"I don't know how else I would describe it." She sighed heavily. "I thought I was imagining it at first. I even tripped and fell on the side of the bed the first time it happened."

"The first time?" He opened his eyes wider. "What did You think You heard?"

"I heard someone thinking *'Please, please let her be alright.'* I could still recall the worry in that voice." She tried to move, succeeding this time because of the shock that rocked Perseus. She rose on her elbows, with one hand slipping and landing in the icy water. "You're lying in the stream?!? Why didn't You say anything before?!?"

"I didn't think it mattered..."

"You cannot lie in the water! You'll catch a cold!" She protested, rising to her feet. Or, at least attempting to do so because she slipped once more, landing atop him for the second time.

"That's one way of helping us get out of this situation." He grinned, wincing from pain, and pretended to be hurt more than he was.

"What situation?" She mumbled while trying to move her hair away from her face to see him better.

"This..." Perseus sighed, whispering the last letter against her lips, with his hand tangled in her hair.

'Oh, my stars...'

Her thoughts mixed with his. They morphed into a single thought, just as her breath caught alongside his. Though she felt numb at first, caught off guard by his gesture, she cupped his bearded cheeks, hoping for more. Hoping for a longer kiss. Hoping to be held by him for a while longer.

"Andromeda..."

"Why did You stop?" She whispered back, with her head spinning. "Did I stop it?"

"No." He caressed the strands of her hair away. "Do You think it's a good idea?"

"What is?" She tipped her head back. "Us falling? Us kissing? Or us pretending not to be attracted to one another?"

"All of the above," he chuckled. "I don't want You to think I took advantage of You being stuck here with me."

"This was just a kiss. I've kissed men before." She tried to pretend not to be hurt by his words, though she could not hide her disappointment.

"I know You have. But I don't think You realize what this means to me."

"I think I do. But I don't think we have to worry about it if You don't intend to kiss me again."

"Then I guess we might have a problem." He clicked his tongue, pulling her in for a kiss she knew - and hoped - was coming...

Chapter 20

So much for history *not* repeating itself...

Sitting in his seasoned chair of the underground office, Perseus scoffed under his nose. There he was, ironically, reaching for the button activating the monitor that would soon connect him with his sister Luna. For the second time that same evening.

Not only was he about to confirm the no longer doubtful possibility of Andromeda's gaining the ability to read minds, but he was also now faced with the frightening reality of having to advise Tom of it as well. And that scared him more than locking lips with Andromeda. Not that he would ever admit it to any of his siblings, and especially to J.J. Monroe.

Alan's presence during the call did not ease the nagging feeling in the pit of his stomach, either.

"Back so soon?" Luna's sleepy voice greeted Perseus.

"Enjoyed nap time, I presume?" Perseus smiled, sending a content nod Alan's way.

"You bet." Luna winked, sitting in her office chair at the Boston residence. "I could have sworn I had gotten used to these baby hormones. But having J.J. around these few days means I get to sleep in a few more times a day."

"Then I am glad You only had to appear a few times in the Big City beside Monroe," Perseus smirked.

"You and me both," she patted her pregnant belly. "Keeping a low profile is a good thing for the First Lady, but when duty calls, it really does."

"I am sure Leo running for the Presidency in this coming election will free up J.J.'s schedule." Alan leaned on the back of Perseus's chair. "Will he be staying in Boston with You longer?"

"He pre-recorded the New Year Address before leaving the Oval Office yesterday. Hopefully, the coming week passes uneventfully. He's due back in D.C. in two days." Saying so, Luna leaned in toward the monitor, narrowing her eyes. "Nap times and my husband's chivalry aside, is there a reason why You are calling back so soon?"

"Yes." Perseus replied in short. Their eldest brother Tom may have possessed the greatest gift of reading minds, but their sister Luna was even more keen on details. And just as suspicious of people's intentions. "We have a problem."

"I'd say two," Alan added, earning a warning gaze from Perseus.

"Two?" Luna raised her eyebrows.

"Just one." Perseus looked back at her.

"What's the second problem?" Luna leaned in a bit closer. She anticipated the reason behind her brother's call but was surprised by Alan's comment.

"What second problem?" J.J. inquired as he walked into the office, closing the door behind him, locking it. This raised Luna's suspicion, and concern all the more.

"I have yet to find out, but Alan said we have two problems," Luna explained.

"I cannot wait to find out, because I think I just found a third one," J.J. advised them in a not-so-stoic tone.

"We do not have two problems." Perseus shook his head.

"I don't, but You do." Alan inclined his head toward his best friend.

"I don't." Perseus grit his teeth.

"Mind telling us what those are? And let us decide if You have a problem or not?" J.J. retorted, intrigued. "Then I'll throw in my two cents and will share what I found out about Your buddy Stoyan Natan."

"How were You able to find out anything so soon?" Luna wondered, impressed.

"Your man has Top Clearence," J.J. straightened his back with pride. "A couple of calls and I got what Perseus asked for."

"Calling Gunay for help does not require Top Clearence," Luna grimaced, mocking him.

"Ouch," Perseus laughed. "Serves You right for asking an Alistair for help."

"Not cool," J.J. brooded. "So, going back to Your problems. What problems did You come across?"

"Only one," Perseus replied in a cool tone. "I was right. Andromeda can read minds."

"Double damn..." J.J. whispered.

"I'm sure Tom will have a harsher response to hearing that," Luna folded her hands.

"Well, he's the one who told me to rush to Andromeda's aid with the linctus vial," Perseus tried to turn the conversation away from him. It failed.

"That's not how I remember it," Alan protested.

"And I doubt Tom will agree to take the blame for it either." Luna sat back in her chair.

"Vega? Admit any fault? Forget about it," J.J. crossed his arms at his chest.

"I thought so," Perseus sighed, resigned, and rubbed his eyes.

"Maybe if You soften the blow with that second problem You stand a chance of appealing to his kind side," Luna suggested.

"I don't think so," Alan winked her way. "Perseus kissed Andromeda."

"You did?" Luna and J.J. grinned in unison.

"I did not!" Perseus protested, with hands frozen mid-movement by his face. "It was an accident."

"That's a foul mouth You have there, Alistair." J.J. scolded him, visibly displeased. "How cowardly of You. You kiss a woman and then refer to it as an accident? If Tom won't punch You, then I will."

"But it was an accident!" Perseus raised his hands. "We stood by the stream, arguing. She tripped, I slipped, and we tumbled to the ground, ending up in the stream."

"How romantic!" Luna clasped her hands.

"It wasn't," Perseus frowned.

"Maybe not the first kiss, but the second one..." Alan chimed in.

"Second one?" Luna and J.J. asked, in unison once more.

"Whose side are You on?" Perseus berated Alan.

"Yours." Alan patted Perseus's shoulder.

"Wait until Gunay finds out." Luna smirked at J.J. with delight.

"He won't." Perseus protested.

"Oh, so he's good for obtaining information about some lowlife poor excuse of a husband, but not good enough for a spicy bout of gossip?" J.J. mocked him.

"I did not ask You to reach out to Gunay, and sure as hell won't stand by while You gossip at my expense." Perseus rose to his feet, overcome with anger.

"It's not gossip. It is out of concern for Your love life," Luna explained, though Perseus saw through her sarcasm.

"I don't have a love life!" Perseus exclaimed so angrily it caused Alan to bite his lip to stop a coming grin.

"We know." Luna chuckled. "You should get one. It does wonders on Your temper."

"Whatever." Perseus puffed out air, perfectly aware he could never win an argument with his sister. "Change of subject. What did You find out from Gunay?"

"That he thinks You should get a love life." J.J. flashed his pearly whites, delivering the line with his usual perfectly stoic tone.

"Monroe!" Perseus hissed out, not amused in the least.

"Sorry," J.J. raised his hands. "Can't blame a brother-in-law for taking a jab at You."

"Remember that next time Rasalas visits You," Perseus mocked him.

"Damn," J.J. whispered, swallowing hard.

"Exactly," Perseus clicked his tongue. "Now, what did You find out from Gunay?"

"Well, for one, he's better than my guys at the White House." J.J. leaned in, moving Luna to the side to access the computer keyboard. Clicking a string of keys, he straightened up after pressing the ENTER key with overstated finesse. "Here is the info on Your buddy Natan."

"He's not my buddy." Perseus countered, sitting down in his chair. He gazed at the photograph displayed on the monitor of the man he came across the day he met Andromeda. "Well, he looked better down on his face."

"Ouch," Alan winced.

"He probably said the same thing," J.J. looked at Luna.

"Well, he does look like someone You would not want to double cross," Luna shrugged. "Or someone You would choose to share Your life with."

"Not everyone is as lucky as You," Alan smiled at Luna.

"Aww. Thank You Alan," Luna mushed, looking up at her husband.

"I second that motion," J.J. smiled, turning his gaze at Perseus. "Andromeda Angelis could not have chosen worse."

"Stoyan Natan was..." Luna read the information displayed on the monitor, raising her hand to her lips. She turned to J.J. in disbelief. "You cannot be serious?"

"Dead serious." J.J. nodded, not surprised by Luna's response. His response had been just as worrisome.

"He was... the son of one of the double agents our parents exposed?" Perseus whispered, reading the words on the screen with a sick feeling in the pit of his stomach...

Chapter 21

Richard and Jade Alistair were good people. They believed in integrity, honor, and judgment grounded on the good side of the law. They chose to devote their lives to exposing those who dared to bend or break the law for greedy selfish reasons.

They raised their children to always seek the right path in life because they realized early on that each of their children were born with unique traits. Their own abilities. Their own strengths which they believed should be used for good and not for bad intentions.

As for their side of how life turned out, the Alistair siblings never gave up on searching for the truth about their parents' passing - staged passing as they have learned recently. Truth which was becoming increasingly complex with every detail about the day their lives changed forever...

"Is everything alright?" Kai asked shyly as he approached Perseus sitting in a seasoned recliner covered with a handmade wool blanket in the kitchen, beside the Christmas tree one morning. Nearly a week had gone by since Perseus learned about the boys' father's identity, and the man's possible connection with his own parents. And the more he thought of it, the more it bothered him.

"Yes." Perseus nodded, thrown off a bit by the boy's question. "Why do You ask?"

"You're usually silent, but today Your eyes are silent too," Kai explained, feeling awkward because of Perseus's reaction.

"My eyes are silent?" Perseus repeated the boy's explanation.

"He's very nosy." Liam tried to defend his brother, though quite unnecessarily.

"Curiosity is a gift many overlook, and even more underestimate," Perseus offered Liam a light smile. "I have a lot on my mind. I like to be quiet when I ponder on things. Kai must have noticed."

"What makes You ponder on things?" Kai asked, glad he had not gotten in trouble.

"Kai!" Liam protested this time.

"What?" Kai turned to his brother. "You ponder on things all the time. It gets annoying. And You never talk about it. At least now I can talk to someone else."

"You like to ponder?" Perseus inquired, putting Liam on the spot. Just as he thought, the boy turned inward the moment he was put on the spot.

"I..." Liam's shoulders hunched. "Sometimes."

"What do You ponder on?" Perseus leaned forward.

"Things." was all Liam said.

"See? I told You." Kai pointed to his brother, triumphant, rolling his eyes. "He's the nosy one, but he never talks about what bugs him."

"Why would You assume that the things he ponders on bug him?" Perseus raised his eyebrow, intrigued.

"Because I know about the things that bug him, but he doesn't want to talk about it." Kai explained with a nod.

"Yeah?" Liam raised his voice a bit. "And what bugs me?"

"I do." Kai flashed him a smile, pleased even more when Perseus let out an unexpected laugh.

"You do bug me, but I never ponder on things that have to do with You." Liam puffed out air, annoyed.

"That's a lie." Kai mocked his brother.

"It is not." Liam narrowed his eyes on Kai, earning a chuckle from Perseus.

"You boys remind me of my brothers," Perseus said before he could think. Then he paused, realizing he unintentionally spoke of his brothers, which caused him to fall silent again.

"We remind You of Gunay and Tom?" Kai inquired with curiosity, sending a shocked jolt of fear down Perseus's spine.

"How do You know their names?" Perseus asked with such urgency it caught Liam's attention.

"You... said their names the day we hid in You shed, when You carried mother inside the cottage?" Liam asked slowly. Too slow for Perseus not to notice. Even though the child did not formulate thoughts, he knew what Liam implied. "You said You had to call them."

"I did, didn't I?" Perseus agreed, aware children often possessed an honesty compass. Had he lied about it, Liam would have noticed, which would cause him to come up with even more questions.

"Yes, You did." Kai straightened up.

"Gunay and Tom are my brothers. And they can be *very* annoying." Perseus sat back in the recliner, hoping the conversation would end there. It did not.

"Who's older?" Liam wondered aloud.

"What?" Perseus replied, neither surprised by the boy's inquisitiveness nor glad about the question. "Why do You ask?"

"Because You don't act like the oldest brother. And You don't act like the youngest one, either." Liam noted.

"And how do I act?" Perseus leaned forward once more.

"You act like an only child, which is odd." Liam retorted in an almost scientific matter-of-fact tone.

"Why odd?" Perseus adjusted in his seat, feeling uncomfortable not because of the line of questions, but by the accuracy of Liam's observation.

"You mentioned Your brothers before, but You act like everything rests on Your shoulders," Liam explained in the same stoic tone, unaware of how much his words affected Perseus.

"That's quite a ponder, young man." Perseus nodded and pointed at the boy. "But I would say back at You."

"So, You agree with me?" Liam grinned from ear to ear.

125

"I do." Perseus grinned as well. "Especially when it comes to people pondering on things that bug them."

"Ha! Told You!" Kai proclaimed victory, catching Perseus off guard by plopping down on the side of the recliner, thereby unexpectedly and unconsciously signaling to Perseus he felt safe around him.

"So, what bugs You so much that You have to ponder about it?" Perseus switched the subject to the first thing that came to his mind, putting Liam on the spot once more.

"Our future." Liam whispered reluctantly, looking at a paper Christmas ornament he had cut out himself. "And... the past."

"I see." Perseus sighed, recognizing so much of himself in the boy sitting on the floor beside the Christmas tree decorated with handmade ornaments made by the boys a few days prior. "And do You like to ponder on things to figure stuff out, or to just reminisce about them?"

"Is there a difference?" Liam looked at him with so much sadness in his eyes it struck a chord in Perseus.

"Yes." Perseus inclined his head. "Sometimes pondering brings back memories of the good times we hope to remember."

"Not all memories are about good times." Liam saddened, looking back at the cutout of the snowflake with uneven edges.

"True." Perseus agreed with him even though it pained him to do so. "But not all of them are sad, either."

"No..." Liam whispered.

"And not all ponderings are about memories," Perseus added, oddly moved to bring some peace to Liam. "Some ponderings, for instance, are about coming up with ways to cause mischief and making sure Your brothers get blamed for it in the end."

"You do that too?" Kai declared.

"What does he do?" Andromeda inquired, intrigued, as she walked in from the outside alongside Tristan.

"He shows he cares for both of his brothers," Perseus clicked his tongue, covering smoothly for both him and Liam. He rose to his feet and set the kettle.

"Liam is a very good brother." Kai smiled from ear to ear as Andromeda looked his way with approval, immediately following with a tongue stuck out at Liam behind her back once Andromeda looked back at Tristan.

"I'm sure." Andromeda shook her head. She hung the jacket beside the door and shook the snow off her hair. "I could use a cup of hot tea or a bowl of hearty stew. Maybe Alan could help me prepare it? Do You think Alan will join us today? He mentioned he would be back yesterday, but he has not returned for a visit."

"I am sure he will stop by. It's unlike him to stay away for more than a day, even in this weather," Perseus replied, seemingly unbothered on the outside. Inside, however, it was a different story.

'Why was he so bothered by what Monroe found...?'

"Boys, Perseus and I will step outside for a moment. Can You please make us some tea?" Andromeda asked Tristan, sending Perseus a direct gaze.

"I think I had enough fresh air. I was outside when the sun rose." Perseus placed his hands at his hips in a sign of protest.

"You could use some more," she replied, zipping up her jacket again.

"I could?" Perseus raised his eyebrow.

"You could, and You should." She walked over to the front door.

"Is Your mother always this bossy?" Perseus looked at Kai.

"She is." Kai agreed in a heartbeat.

"I guess I have no choice then." Perseus grimaced, and walked out onto the front porch, grabbing his jacket. He donned the jacket, zipped it up, and made his way toward Andromeda under the covered porch on the side of the cottage. "Alright, what's up? I don't need any more fresh air. So, why did You make an excuse for me to follow You? Was it because You missed kissing me?"

Andromeda turned to face him so suddenly Perseus took a step back. Not only did he not anticipate her move this fast, but he also did not expect her question. "Who's Monroe...?"

Chapter 22

"Who???"

Perseus swallowed hard, barely uttering the three letters as a cold sweat rolled down his back. Hadn't he just verified to his sister that the woman standing before him did in fact acquire the ability to read minds? Yes, he did. But he forgot the number one assassin rule - to never let one's guard down. He did. He admitted doing so. And he cursed himself for it.

He now faced two challenges he knew he could not fail at. One: making damn sure he raised that guard back up along with making double damn sure to block Andromeda from reading his mind again. And two: coming up with a sound explanation as to who Monroe was - without revealing more than he had to.

He just did not anticipate how revealing the half-truths would further complicate his life - and everyone's future...

"Monroe." Andromeda repeated the name, puzzled by Perseus's pale-faced grimace and fear-filled eyes.

"Why do You ask?" Perseus narrowed his eyes, pretending he had no idea what she meant.

"Why are You so offended by the question?" She narrowed her eyes as well, matching his suspicious gaze.

"Why shouldn't I be?"

"Why would You feel the need to do so?"

"You read my mind without my permission." His explanation was a sound one, though incomplete.

"Wait, You didn't say that out loud?" Andromeda opened her eyes wide.

"I..." Perseus panicked, with hair raising at the small of his neck. He swore on the inside. True, Andromeda may have gained mind-reading abilities, but she knew next to nothing about how it worked. And now he was faced with yet another challenge: would he pretend not to know exactly how it worked, or would he help her to figure it out - but in doing so reveal his ability to read minds as well? "I did not say anything out loud. You must have read my mind and did not bother to think if it was appropriate or not."

"How was I supposed to know You just thought those words?" She pointed at him, defiant, poking his chest. "I did not choose to be poisoned. And I sure did not choose to be left with the poison's side effects."

"I..." Perseus calmed down considerably. If she really did choose to attribute the sudden onset of mind-reading ability to being poisoned, she saved him from having to come up with some farfetched excuse neither of them would have been satisfied with. "I guess my accusation was a bit blown out of proportion."

"A bit blown out of proportions?" She scoffed. "I'm dealing with these new voices in my head. I don't want to have to deal with Your attitude any more than I have to."

"I don't have an attitude." He chuckled, amused, and somehow not as bothered as he would have been not long ago.

"You don't?" She mocked him. "Then how do You explain Alan's absence? What did You do to that sweet man?"

"Oh, so I have an attitude yet he's a sweet man?" Perseus poked her shoulder. "You should check Your attitude before You judge those around You."

"Fine," she flashed him a quick insincere smile which disappeared faster than it appeared. "But You must have done something to Alan to make him stay away these past few days."

"Maybe it was You?"

"Never." She shook her head. "Alan adores us. I would never do anything to upset him."

"Sure." Perseus agreed. "You just prefer to upset me."

"It goes both ways." She took a step away, turning to face the stream glistening in the glory of the mountain sun, opting to cross her hands at her chest rather than allowing the conversation to go deeper on that topic.

"I guess You are right," Perseus nodded, sending her an alluring - and completely ineffective gaze. "Though I must admit I could go for a spat or two in the snow - or an icy stream."

"Forget it," she replied too fast, and therefore hinting to Perseus to read her thoughts.

'I could not let that happen...'

"Why?" He asked before he could stop himself and knew at once he would need to come up with a cover up. He offered an explanation she barely accepted. "The ground is still covered with snow, with more of it coming tomorrow. I'd say we go for it and blame it on the slippery fluff."

"No." She shook her head. "Besides, You still did not explain who Monroe is?"

"You still insist on knowing?" Perseus sighed. He needed to decide then and there whether lying or revealing the truth would prove best in the situation. And then he recalled the consequences that followed when Caelum lied to them when it came to Emmeline. He sighed again. He was not a liar. He would reveal what little truth he needed to reveal, but he would not lie. Not when it mattered. Because it mattered. "Monroe is a friend of mine."

"Is he more of a friend than Alan?" She countered his response and did so in a way that struck a chord in Perseus's gut.

"Why would You ask me that?"

"I may have read Your mind unintentionally, but I did read it, nonetheless. And You did mention Alan was bothered by something Your friend Monroe found." She turned back toward him. "I may be crossing a line here - again - but I hope whatever Your friend said he found did not hurt Alan."

"Well, to be honest, Monroe is a good friend of mine, but Alan matters to me more than I could put into words," and he meant it. "Alan saved my life. That is not something I take lightly."

"How did he save it?"

"Up there, in the mountains." He nudged his head toward the mountains towering around them. "When I met him years ago, he was part of the Tatra Volunteer Search and Rescue. That's how I got involved with them."

"And I guess speaking English was a plus for them, huh?" She looked in the direction of the mountains imagining Alan as a volunteer in the past.

"You might say that. My Polish is as broken as my manners, but many around here speak English. And it is a plus because of the tourist business," he smirked. "Your English is pretty good, too, if I may say so."

"I was born in England," she explained. "When my family died, I couldn't stay where we lived. I just couldn't. So, I may or may not have snuck in on one of the boats passing from England to the mainland. And I eventually ended up here, just across the mountains."

"I know the feeling." Perseus sighed. And immediately swore on the inside. He knew the woman standing before him for only a short while. He never intended to reveal to her any information about who he was, or about his past, or about his family. But he said what he said, and words once spoken could never be taken back. "Do You recall the way I lost my temper when You mentioned my parents?"

"How could I forget? Though I must say the consequences more than overcompensated for it."

"I'll say." He wiggled his eyebrows, then grew silent. "I lost my parents years ago. I still can't get over that feeling of helplessness and despair."

"It stays with You, doesn't it?" She reached for him, touching his forearm.

"That, it does."

"Is that why You ended up in this place? Far from everyone?"

"More or less," he retorted, somehow calmer because her presence soothed his broken spirit. "This was Alan's place. He offered it to me. And gave me space because he understood I needed it more than physical healing from my injuries."

"If he cares about You so much, whatever this Monroe guy said must have been significant if it caused him to stay away?"

"I guess. What Monroe said shocked me. It made me sick. It made me think of a dozen ways to retaliate against those to whom the information pertained. But I cannot figure out why Alan just left without a word."

"Retaliate?" Andromeda retrieved her hand. "That sounds vindictive."

"And it felt that way." He leaned against the wooden porch post of the staircase leading off the porch. "You'd have felt the same way if You heard it."

"I might, if You cared enough to share it with me."

"I care."

"Then allow me to care as well," she smiled shyly. "What exactly did Your friend Monroe say?"

"He said Stoyan Natan was the son of the man who may have been responsible for my parents' untimely passing..."

≈ Chapter 23 ≈

If Perseus had to guess, he would bet his assassin's salary that the words which spilled out of his mouth affected Andromeda as much as they affected him. But he did not need to guess, though. He knew. And not because he could read minds.

He knew because he understood how earthshattering it felt to be blindsided.

What made it worse, or more significant, was the fact the woman gazing at him with a blank stare wasn't someone he did not care about. He could not pinpoint how it happened, and heavens knew he could not figure out exactly when. But he began to care about Andromeda, even if he found it hard to admit. Especially when the way she was looking at him said more than he was willing to accept. She cared, too. He felt it. Not just about him. She cared about what happened to his parents.

And *THAT* he could not dismiss...

"What... do You mean?" She choked up, shocked. "Stoyan was no saint, but do You honestly think he was capable of killing Your parents?"

"He did come after You, didn't he? The poison didn't exactly get to Your blood by itself." Perseus explained, not moving an inch. "But I did not say he was the one responsible for my parents' passing. It looks like his father was."

"Are You sure?" She whispered, taken aback not only by the information, but also by the impossible likelihood of their lives somehow being connected.

"No, I am not. But Monroe is."

"Is he?"

"Yes."

"How in the world was Your friend able to find the information so quickly? I just told You who my deceased husband was a few days ago. Is this Monroe guy that good?" She tipped her head.

"He is." Perseus admitted, deciding against admitting Gunay's involvement in obtaining the information.

"How did he do it so fast?"

"He's got friends with connections," he replied, biting his tongue because he realized he was already revealing too much.

"Does he?"

"Yes."

"If You don't mind me asking, do You trust him?"

"I do."

"You do? Why?"

"Because the man who found and verified the information was my brother Gunay," he opted to reveal the truth, nonetheless. "Monroe just conveyed the intel."

"Intel?" She chuckled anxiously. "What are You? A spy?"

"No."

"Is Monroe?"

"Damn, no!" Perseus denied at once. "And he'd take that accusation as an insult."

"Why?"

"Because he is a righteous guy."

"Are You?"

"You really have to ask me that?" He grimaced, offended.

"Yes, I do."

"Why?"

"Because I care about my sons' safety." She tipped her head up, unaware she exposed herself to Perseus's intention of reading her mind. He did. And was hit with a wave of feelings he was not ready for.

'Because I care about YOU...'

"Well, damn..." he whispered with a knot twisting his gut.

"Well, damn?" She raised her hands. "Did You think I would not care about my sons?"

"That's not what I meant," he shook his head, and watched as she slowly brought her hands up to her lips, covering them.

"Did... You read my mind?!? How?!?"

"What?" He blinked.

"You must have." She hesitated. "But how?"

"How what?" He mumbled, anticipating her next question, fully aware he was too panicked to reply honestly.

"How did You read my mind?"

"What are You talking about?" He took his steps around her, walking off the porch to put more distance between them.

"Did You react to what I said? Or to what I thought?" She caught up with him, stepping in front of him.

"Don't be ridiculous. I heard what You said." He stood his ground. It was burning at his feet, but he knew he had to evade the question - or rather evade the real answer to it. "Did Your thoughts not match what You said?"

"No, they did not!" She raised her voice.

"Why?"

"Why what?"

"Why didn't Your words match Your thoughts?" He touched the lapel of her jacket, showing her he was winning the argument. "Don't You care about Your sons' safety?"

"Of course, I do!"

"Then what were You thinking that did not match Your statement?"

"I... I thought about You," she lowered her voice.

"Oh? And why did You automatically accuse me of this silly idea of me reading Your thoughts? Did You feel guilty about thinking of me?"

"No. Besides, it means nothing. And don't change the subject," she pointed at him. "We were talking about Stoyan."

"You are right. Because talking about Your thoughts - or feelings - toward me is not relevant." He exhaled, glad to have moved past the idea of his mind-reading ability.

"Not right now." She retrieved her hand. "Exactly what did Your brother find out about Stoyan's father?"

"Not much. Only that somehow, someway, his father may have played a part in the way my parents met their end."

"May have?"

"Did."

"Did the Police investigation mention anything about him?" She tried to take a step toward him, but he walked away, closer to the stream.

"What Police investigation?" He scoffed, looking toward the mountaintops. "Sometimes Cold Cases are just that. Cold."

"I'm sorry." She tried to comfort him, unaware of how deep his sorrow reached. Or how much it still stung not being able to have done anything about it.

"So am I. At least You know where Your family is buried."

"What?"

"Exactly that..." he fell silent, neither turning toward her nor admitting without guilt that he said more than he should have.

"Their bodies were never found?"

"Not only that. We didn't even find out where they died."

"But if that's true, how could You be sure they died in the first place?" The question, however innocent in its nature, tugged at his conscience.

"Because we were told they did." Perseus sighed, feeling the rush of anger building up inside him. It wasn't an anger directed at her - it was directed at himself. She just happened to ignite it.

"And You never questioned it?"

"The hell we didn't!" He turned to her now, his eyes shining with resentment and pain. "I spent years searching for clues, signs, any kind of information pertaining to their end. We all did. Not a day goes by that I don't fall asleep with guilt weighing heavy on my heart."

"Guilt? Why on earth would You feel guilty about it?"

"Yes, why would You?" Alan repeated Andromeda's words, startling her and Perseus.

"You're back!" Andromeda cheered up and made her way to greet him. "We missed You."

"As I missed You, dear. You and Your boys." Alan inclined his head with the grace of a seasoned gentleman and patted her hand.

"Didn't miss me, then? " Perseus sent Alan a half-grin.

"I did, but You don't smile this wide when I visit. Nor do You do so with this much warmth."

"I'll smile wider next time." Perseus winked at him, but Alan noticed the grim look in his eyes.

"What happened?" Alan walked up to Perseus, concerned.

"You didn't come by for a couple days. We worried," Perseus moved his shoulders.

"And I worried it was because of us," Andromeda noted.

"You worried unnecessarily, my dear," Alan inclined his head toward her.

"Maybe so." Andromeda linked her hand through Alan's arm. "But I hope the information You heard from Monroe about my ex-husband's connection to whatever may have happened to Perseus's parents did not keep You away?"

"You know about Monroe?" Alan asked her, astonished, and looked at Perseus. "You told her about Your parents, too?"

"I told her about what Monroe told us," Perseus advised him.

"I see." Alan nodded in understanding, and unfortunately, so did Andromeda.

"Is there more?" She narrowed her eyes on Perseus. "I may read minds now, but I cannot do so if someone refuses to share their thoughts."

"Well, now." Alan tried to appear surprised. "What do You mean You may read minds?"

"I can." she nodded. "We figured it was a side effect of the poison I was injected with."

"We?" Alan inquired, taking a suspicious look at Perseus.

"We." Was all Perseus said. It was all he could say given the circumstances.

"Did You figure out if it will go away?" Alan wondered, with hair raising at the small of Perseus's neck.

"I... kind of hope it won't," Andromeda smiled.

"You do?" Alan smirked with mischief, doubling the fear bubbling up in Perseus's gut.

"I do." Andromeda continued to smile.

"Then I suggest Perseus takes You on a little morning stroll. If You read minds as much as You think You do, You might as well put it to the test." Alan sent Perseus a smug grin, patted his arm in a not-so-innocent brotherly manner, and turned to walk toward the cabin fully aware of the invisible arrows his best friend surely considered firing his way...

≈ **Chapter 24** ≈

Vexed at first by Alan's idea of taking a morning stroll with Andromeda, Perseus soon reconsidered it. The further they walked away from his cabin, the more relaxed he felt.

Maybe he needed the unspoken freedom the mountains towering around them offered? Maybe he needed the serenity of the silence echoing through the mountain peaks? Or maybe he yearned for peace of the undisturbed unbeaten paths within the snow-covered trees only he was aware of?

Leaving Alan in charge of Andromeda's sons for a few good hours wasn't the problem. Convincing her sons their mother was well enough to undertake an hours-long outing was. Especially when it came to Tristan...

"Your sons love You very much." Perseus kept their conversation light and at minimum to ensure she did not waste too much energy.

"They do." She smiled with rays of the high-noon January sun caressing her cheeks. Although the day called for brisk wintery weather, she felt as if the cloudless cerulean sky itself invited her for the hike. "I don't know what I'd have done if Stoyan would have taken them away from me."

"He didn't." Perseus retorted, not at all saddened that his first encounter with the lowlife loser was his last. "And he never will."

"I'd like to believe it. I have to believe it." She sighed, though the exhaled breath had little in common with relief of the built-up ball of nerves she kept to herself. "He's gone, but I doubt his men will not seek revenge against us."

"Let me worry about that." He sent her a direct gaze, one she could see even through the blue polarized aviator sunglasses Perseus insisted they'd wear.

"There's that misplaced hero complex," she chuckled while she followed him in the undisturbed snow way off the tourist path.

"Not funny." He paused at half-step, causing Andromeda to stop at the last moment in an attempt not to ram into him. She barely succeeded. "Besides, for all we know his men might have already assumed such a fragile Milksop, not to mention Your sons, would have perished in the mountains days ago."

"Did You just call me a Milksop?" Now she paused, with her mitten-covered hands at her hips.

"Yes." He winked. "I also called You fragile."

"Rude!"

"No such thing." He whirled around and pointed back at her with a gloved-up hand. "But You must have missed the part where I said that it was Your halfwit of ex-husband's men who thought of You in those terms."

"Sure." She kept her hands at her hips but resumed walking and caught up with him. "You must have missed the part where I cared about Your caveman opinion."

"Of course, You do. Otherwise, You'd have been unaffected by my reference to a Milksop." He winked again. "Nevertheless, I am glad Tristan didn't put up a fistfight at the idea of us taking this longer hike."

"He's protective of me. Can You blame him? I'm all he has now."

"He has his brothers, too."

"That's true, but it's not the same. Siblings may offer support in times of sorrow, but a parent is and always will be a parent. No amount of sibling love will compensate for it."

"You're right."

"I'm sorry. I did not mean to make You sad."

"I know."

"I hope one day You will get the closure You are seeking."

"That makes two of us."

"Then I also hope whatever else this Monroe friend of Yours is able to uncover about Stoyan's father's connection to Your parents ends up leading us to the truth." She meant those words as well. And that got to him.

"Us?"

"Yes," she replied without hesitation. "I want to get to the bottom of it as much as You do. Does that... bother You?"

"No." He replied without conviction. Too quick for her not to notice it, too dry-toned for her to believe him.

"And yet, it does?" She noted, debating whether to put her mind-reading skills to the test like Alan suggested.

"Think what You must, it's not illegal." He sent her a smile which did not look convincing. So, he circled around to the one topic he knew Andromeda would focus on. Tristan. "Seriously, though, I was impressed with the way Tristan figured out that the hike would prove beneficial for You. We have to make sure You are getting stronger."

"We?" She repeated after him, and received a full-blown smile because Perseus realized she played on words the same way he did a moment ago.

"Yes."

"Alright. In that case, You might want to pick up Your Milksop pace. I don't know where we are going. I don't mind getting there, but I do mind doing so after sundown. This isn't exactly a walk on a beach."

"Point taken, though it might surprise You that our destination has a lot to do with the beach," he clicked his tongue, pointing at her.

"And where do You suppose we'll find a beach in the Tatra Mountains?" She laughed, with the sound echoing around them.

'Ahh, shit...'

His thoughts, however discrete and personal, rang loud and clear in her mind. And she just had to mention it.

"Must You use that kind of language around me?"

"What?" He stopped, staring at her. "Did You just read my mind *again?*"

"Yes." She admitted. There was no point in denying it. "Alan did say You were to take me out on this little stroll so I could figure out how well I can read Your mind, didn't he?"

"Some best friend." Perseus rolled his eyes.

"That, he is." She grinned. "And I do believe he meant well to suggest it."

"I don't."

"Why did You think what You just thought?"

"I tripped over a tree branch sticking out of the snow."

"I see no branch?" She looked down by his feet.

"Just because You can't see it doesn't mean it's not there."

She took a decisive step forward, closing the distance between them. He stood his ground. If he didn't, he was sure he would have lost his footing - branch or no branch. "What else am I not seeing?"

'Ahh, damn...'

His next thought was that of a swear word. Not because his mind grew blank. It was because all he could see was his reflection in her sunglasses, glaring at him, with the deep blue sky and rays of the sun shining above them.

"Damn?" She flashed her pearly whites aware she was getting under his skin. Feeling even better, she wiggled her eyebrows, and slowly formed a smug grin.

'Double damn...'

How on earth was he supposed to concentrate on anything other than those lips of hers? So plump from the cold... So skimmed by the sun...

"So eager to kiss?" Was all she had to whisper to shake him back to reality.

"Ahh, shit."

"So, that's why You thought what You thought?"

"You're playing with fire, Milksop."

"Who said anything about playing? When it comes to kissing, I NEVER play."

She pulled him in and kissed him. Passionately. Hastily. Breathlessly. Whether it was the urge to press her lips to his. Whether it was the urge to grab hold of the straps of his hiking backpack. Whether it was the way he challenged her. It did not matter. Then again, all of it mattered. And by the time she pulled her lips back, she was certain his mind was as blank as hers.

"Double damn." He muttered after a moment.

"Got that right!" She clicked her tongue, pointing at him as she past him. "Remember that next time You accuse me of playing."

He nodded, shaking his head slowly. He pulled himself together, blocking his thoughts from her. And swore on the inside. How was he supposed to keep that guard up if she kept surprising him left and right? No more. Not this time, and not again.

"You never told me where we're hiking?" She asked, her voice still playful and witty.

"The Eye of the Sea. We're heading to the Eye of the Sea," he said as he caught up with her, whirled her around for a kiss she had not expected, and took the lead in every sense of the word...

≈ Chapter 25 ≈

Standing at the foot of the Eye of the Sea, a serene lake part of the Rybi Potok, the Fish Brook, Andromeda took in the view towering above and in front of them. She always knew the Tatra Mountains were beautiful, but this view took her breath away.

The view of the lake, enclosed by the tall mountains around it as if they were caressing it or keeping it safe with utmost care, offered Andromeda a sense of security. Even with the setting sun far out of their view. Even with the breezy fog rolling down the tree-covered mountain slopes. Even with the realization they weren't the only ones visiting the lake, albeit with other visitors standing near the chalet of the Polish Tourism and Local Lore Society on the opposite shore of the lake.

Especially, because of the presence of others for the first time since her last human encounter when she had been poisoned...

"This was worth the hike, wouldn't You say?" He released a satisfactory sigh of relief and victory, nudging her shoulder.

"It hardly compares to a beach. Though I must say it sure looks beautiful." She smiled, however her gaze remained fixed on the groups of people near the chalet. She hoped he wouldn't have noticed, but that hope faded quickly.

"What's wrong?" His tone carried more worry than curiosity.

"Those people... can they see us?" She pointed across the lake.

"No less than we can see them," he retorted. "But they won't be able to get to us."

"No?" She looked up at him. Since she removed her sunglasses, there was no way to prevent him from seeing the worry in her eyes.

"No. We blend with the surroundings. We're wearing white weatherproof gear so unless they know we're here, they wouldn't bother to look for us." He grinned, taking off his sunglasses. "I know my way around this land. I know half a dozen ways of getting here, and a half a dozen more of the nearest ways out. Plus, it will be dark soon. No one in their right mind would bother to hike to where we are at this hour."

"Speaks a lot about Your decision to come here."

"Ha, not funny." He nudged her once more. "How about You help me with what I brought along in my hiking backpack, and You'll thank me by saying I actually had a good idea."

"You've ever had any?" Teasing him felt good. It felt even better when she realized what he packed. "Point for You. Maybe this wasn't such a bad idea after all."

"Thanks." He handed the other end of a rolled thick white waterproof tarp.

"How long do You intend for us to stay here?"

"Until the stars come out." Saying so, he pulled out a white oversized sleeping bag.

"Are You out of Your mind?" She dropped her arms at her sides, flabbergasted. "I'm not sleeping outside in THIS weather."

"Who said anything about sleeping?" He straightened. "We hiked here for hours. We will rest here for a while, warm up, and then head back. I gave Tristan my word we will return home before morning."

"Morning?!?" The word echoed around them, causing her to hunch her shoulders.

"Yes," he countered with a serious face. "You did intend to test Your mind-reading skills, didn't You?"

"I... guess so."

"Then we agree."

"But morning? We'll freeze here when the sun goes down." She pointed toward the sky. "You can't even see the sun - or the sky for that matter - with all this fog."

148

"That's mountain weather for You. She is moody, capricious, and can with absolute certainty change in a matter of minutes," he noted, pointing to an inner corner of the sleeping bag. "We won't freeze. This sleeping bag is a heated one. Tried and tested. Plus, it's oversized and fits two without a problem."

"Two?" She paused. "How often do You bring women here?"

"Never."

"Your personal life is not something I should pry into. It was just a question."

"I did not mean to offend You." Yet somehow, he felt he did. That was new territory for him. New ground. One he didn't know how to trudge through.

"And I did not mean to do so either." She half-smiled but it did not reach her eyes. "Mind opening that sleeping bag? It has gotten chilly since we stopped moving."

"Oh. Right." He laid the sleeping bag down on the waterproof tarp, took out another - thicker – white tarp and laid it over the sleeping bag, then secured it at the ends. "This should keep us warm and dry until we head back. It's part of my gear when I set out for trekking in the mountains."

"Alright," she nodded. Seeing what he was doing, she followed in his steps. She removed the hiking boots and mittens, placed the mittens inside the boots to keep them warmer, and placed them under the top tarp beside her. Once they settled inside, she began to relax and felt compelled to give credit when credit was due. "Thank You."

"For what?" He wondered and made sure to sit beside her yet not right next to her. She had her boundaries, but he had them as well. He may have taken her to the lake, but she would be the one to decide what would happen.

"For everything." She fell silent. Her gaze traveled across the pond of pitch-black waters contrasting against the mountain slopes covered with pristine white snow.

"For being a knuckleheaded mountain brute, too?"

"Yes," she laughed. She did not expect the gesture to ease so much tension from the small of her neck. Then again, she didn't expect so much to have happened since the day she met him.

"I like it when You do that."

"Do what?"

"Oh, so now You're having trouble reading my mind?"

"Knuckleheaded mountain brute!"

"At Your service. I like when You laugh like that."

"Like what?"

"Unbothered. Sincerely. Happily. I lived with sadness for a long time. It's nice to spend time with someone who still finds joy in life." He sighed, then sighed once more when she scooted closer to him.

"There have been years where I only felt the sadness," she explained, resting her head on his shoulder. "Tristan changed that. He may not be my son, per se, but he reminded me there is still so much light left in the world."

"He is a good young man. I see more of Your wisdom in him than of any anger from his father."

"I hope so. They say You can't pick Your parents, but it doesn't mean we have to follow their path." She closed her eyes. When she opened them, she saw his had teared up. "Perseus? Are You alright?"

"No." He began to tense up, but she turned toward him, caressing his bearded cheek.

"Talk to me about it. About how You feel."

"I... can't." He clenched his jaw out of anger at himself. "I don't have the words."

"If You have feelings built up inside, then You already have the words. It's a matter of deciding whether to share them with me or not."

"We were told they died because I failed them."

"What?" Her hand paused against his cheek. "What do You mean?"

"I failed. I wanted to help them, and they never came back because I failed."

"Never came back?" She repeated after him. "Who?"

"My parents..." he covered his face with his hands.

The battle he fought on the inside was not only that of truth versus lie. It was a battle of pride versus shame. Sorrow versus despair. Holding everything inside versus finally releasing all the emotions he bottled up inside - ones he could never have shared with anyone before, not even with Alan.

"Hey." She adjusted, cupping his face. "We may not know each other for a long time, but You can trust me. I trust You. After all, I wouldn't be here if You hadn't saved me."

"You don't know how dark of a place the world could be when the burden of the past weighs so heavy on the heart."

"I think You and I can agree the past weighs pretty heavy on my heart as well," her eyes softened. "How bad can it be?"

It was now or never. And never proved too much of a burden on his heart. "My parents... Richard and Jade. They were secret agents. They worked to uncover double spies. And they never came back from their last mission because I failed to make my damn tracking device work."

"Perseus..." she caught her breath. "Is that... is that how they may have been connected to Stoyan's father?"

"I don't know." He released a sob filled with sorrow and guilt. "I don't know."

"Look at me. I'm here for You. I am here with You. You can lean on me."

"I can't." He shook his head.

"Why not?"

"Because if I do, I wouldn't know how to turn back..."

"Then don't." Was all she said, bringing his lips to hers...

Chapter 26

When the world stopped spinning, Andromeda found herself lost in her thoughts. She did not know what time it was. She did not know how long they had been kissing. She did not know if she would be fine once their embrace had stopped. She knew, however, that she never felt the way she did about the man whose strong arm made her feel safe and desired.

"It got dark." She noticed as her eyelashes fluttered open ever so slowly.

"Mhm." His eyes opened as well. "Since all I can see is You, I'll trust Your judgment."

"That's because You're lying on top of me."

"I don't mind it if You don't." He tipped his nose to hers, with his hand lost somewhere in her hair under her jacket, the other one supporting her back.

"It may be dark, but I can feel You grinning."

"Well, why not?" Kissing the tip of her nose, he raised himself a bit on one elbow. "It's cozy. We're inside the heated sleeping bag. You're in my arms. And I must say I haven't felt this content in... I'd say forever."

"Content?" She chuckled. "I asked You to share Your thoughts and feelings with me, but all You managed to do is kiss my brain cells away."

"That's possible?"

"Perseus..." she scoffed, pushing her hand against his chest to prevent another slew of kisses.

"What? I happen to think I am a pretty good kisser. Moreover, I would consider sharing *that* profound thought of mine is part of the deal." To make his point, he succeeded in kissing her again.

'You proved Your point...'

She smiled against his lips. How serene and safe it felt to be embraced by someone who valued her, cared for her, cared about her?

"I'm sorry to have made You hike for hours." His tone changed. "This place holds a lot of meaning to me. There aren't many places that do that."

"You like to be alone, don't You?" She caressed the strands of hair around his face with one hand, while her other one shifted to rest on his back, under his unzipped jacket.

"I used to." He inclined his head. "Now, I hope I no longer have to."

"You don't." She cupped his cheek. "And I hope You don't kick us out."

"What if I... ask You to stay longer?"

"Would You?" She asked aloud, but inside it was all she could think of.

'Please, don't make us leave...'

"Andromeda, I..." He wanted to tell her. About all the rest. About everything he was keeping from her. But he was afraid. Very afraid. "There are things about me that would shock You. That's why I have a hard time sharing anything about me or my family."

"Your family?" She wondered, surprised. "But You already told me about Your parents. How much more could there be?"

"More. A lot more." He rolled on his back. The air around them was as clouded as his mind. "I can't see the stars. Just the fog."

"I know." She turned to him and placed her hand on his heart, hoping he would not shut her out.

"If I tell You about me, You have to promise You won't run. It's too dark and Your hiking boots are behind me."

154

"You didn't run from me when You found out about the connection between Your parents and Stoyan's father, did You?"

"You're right." Yet, to be sure she would not run at first instinct, he wrapped his arm around her. "Actually, have You ever met his father? Any information would help me."

"I never got a chance. Stoyan said his father worked somewhere on the other side of the world, and then died before I got a chance to meet him," she paused to recall any details she may have picked up on over the years. "Stoyan would call him every now and then. He never met my three boys, either."

"I won't pretend to feel sorry for him."

"You? Pretend?" She let out a gentle titter, nuzzling closer to him. "You may be a mountain brute, but I doubt You'd be capable of pretending anything. Your face is too honest."

"What?" He grimaced, amused.

"You have an honest face. It reveals a lot. Even if I wouldn't read Your mind, I'd see everything on Your face."

"Oh, really?"

"Yes." She could see little in the dim glow of the snowy slopes around them, but she could see his eyes. "Remember the day You caught Alan and I speaking about Your mother?"

"I do." He did. The mere mention of his mother by Alan jabbed at the wound in his heart.

"Your eyes almost glowed with a mix of temper, fury, and resentment."

"They did?" He felt exactly the way she described it. He did not appreciate that feeling back then. He sure did not feel comfortable thinking of it now.

"Yes," she nodded. "To think of it now, it is that raw honesty that kind of attracted me to You."

"It did?" He embraced her closer... and decided to be honest with her because he realized the walls he built around his heart were of no use against someone who meant so much to him. "Andromeda, I'm an assassin."

He felt her body tense. How could she not? Who wouldn't have, under the circumstances? He knew revealing the truth to her would carry with it consequences. He only hoped she would respect him enough to keep the information to herself if they ever parted ways.

"An assassin?"

"Yes. The choice to follow this path in life did not come lightly, but it was one we had to make."

"We?" Her eyes widened.

"My siblings and I..." he paused, hoping to high heavens he made the right choice of trusting the woman in his arms. It worked for his siblings, except for Rasalas. That mistake cost them dearly, and almost cost Rasalas his life.

"You're assassins?"

"Yes." He admitted. "Well, not all. We all were, but some aren't any longer."

"Is it like a membership You have to renew and their licenses expired?"

She asked so stoically, and with such curiosity, he could not help but laugh. "I reveal my darkest secret to You and You poke fun of it?"

"No such thing. My question was of the most serious sort."

"I bet." He caressed a strand of hair behind her ear and felt the tension ease in her. "So, are You fine with it?"

"I figured there was more to You than just being a rude host."

"I am not a rude host."

"Of course You are," she tsk-tsked. "But I guess living alone with such a burden of truth makes You trust very few."

"It does." He exhaled. Part in relief, part with concern. "Can we try something?"

"What?"

"Can we see if You can read my mind? After all, that's why we came here."

"I thought You'd never ask." She pulled herself up gently, resting on his chest, hands folded on his heart. "Think of something. Anything."

'I like Your smile...'

"You like my smile!" She exclaimed, proud of herself, immediately wincing at the echo of her voice carried across the lake and upwards toward the mountain slopes.

"Good job." he grinned. "How about now?"

'You cook a mean stew...'

"I do cook a mean stew!" She repeated his thoughts with excitement though a bit quieter.

"How about this one?" He narrowed his eyes on her.

'I tripped on purpose that day by the stream. I could not wait to kiss You...'

"I knew it!" Proclaiming a great triumph, aware he took the blame despite knowing she caused the fall, she tickled the lower side of his back. He tensed up immediately. "You're ticklish?"

"No."

"Yes!" She cackled even more triumphantly.

'No...!'

"Really?" She tickled the same spot. His response proved her point. So did his clenched jaw. "Oh, You can bet I'm going to use this knowledge to my advantage."

"Until I find Your tickle spot."

"You're telling me only *that* spot is ticklish?" She let out a mocking and wickedly feminine growl. "Oh, Perseus Alexander, challenge accepted."

"Perseus Alistair. My real name is Perseus Alistair."

"Perseus Alistair," she whispered, allowing him to hear his name coming from a woman he cared about for the first time in his life.

"Andromeda Angelis..." he whispered slowly. His tone changed. His eyes changed. His... life changed in that one heartbeat. He brought her closer to kiss her, but she tensed up.

"I won't ask You to do anything You wouldn't do." Saying so, he released the grip around her waist.

"It's not that. I just..." she began to explain but stopped. "I'm afraid."

"So am I, believe me."

"You don't understand," she shook her head. "I... I am a mother."

"And it is as much a part of You as reading minds now."

"No, that's not what I meant." She shook her head. "I mean, yes, that too, but that's not why I am afraid."

"Then why?"

"I am a mother. I have a mother's figure..."

"And it is a beautiful one."

"But You can clearly see it..." Her voice cracked.

"Not in this dark a night."

"It won't be dark forever," she began to pull back.

"Don't." He held onto her. "How old are You?"

"What?" She tipped her head.

"How old are You? It's a basic question."

"Basic, yes, but one You should never ask a woman," she jabbed at his ribs playfully.

"I just told You I'm an assassin. The least You can do is tell me how old You are."

"I'll be thirty this coming April," she explained, feeling even worse than a moment ago.

"You're older than me," he announced proudly, causing her to gaze at him with a temper.

"Really, Alistair?" She scolded him. "Way to dampen a spirit."

"What I meant..." he turning them around, with her resting under him. "I'm younger. But it doesn't matter."

"Really?" She smirked. "What does, then?"

"Look up," he cupped her face. "The stars are out."

"Oh, Perseus..." she caught her breath. The sight of the night sky ruling above them wrapped an invisible knot around her heart. As did the sight of his eyes, filled with nothing but tenderness and understanding.

"You mean so much to me." He whispered, kissing her forehead. "But there is something else You need to know about me."

"Tell me."

"It's not something I can tell You. It's something I need to let You hear in my thoughts." Saying so, he lowered his lips to hers, and when she didn't pull away, he whispered in his thoughts.

'I can read minds, too...'

≈ **Chapter 27** ≈

Returning home felt like a breeze. Literally. What took hours to hike from the Ku Dziurze Gorge to the Eye of the Sea lake above the ground, took less than half that time to get back home in the underground tunnels Andromeda had never heard of. She just held onto Perseus's hand as they moved in the dark labyrinth of caves in the dim light of their head lamps.

They were coming back changed. Whole. Content. With plenty of time left before sunrise. As odd as it seemed to Andromeda, she felt safe. Safe. Safer than she ever felt in her whole life. Not only because Perseus found a way into her heart, but because he opened his heart to her as well. And he revealed so much of his private life she was barely able to comprehend the severity of it all.

He was an assassin.

A mind-reading assassin.

His parents' disappearance was somehow linked to her deceased father-in-law whom she never met. Disappearance, because Perseus also revealed his parents somehow survived an ambush meant to end their lives...

"I thought my life had twisted knots. You sure know how to one-up somebody." She nudged Perseus as they emerged from one of the tunnel entrances not far from his cottage.

"Do You still think of me as a self-centered Mountain Man macho with a misplaced hero syndrome?" He wrapped his arm around her as they walked toward the cottage in the starry night after emerging from the caves.

"Do I ever!" She replied with cheer. "But at least now I know there is so much more to You."

"Wicked woman," he embraced her tighter. "Does it bother You I just dumped all this information on Your shoulders?"

"No. I value trust. And since You trusted me with all of it, then I shall have enough in me to bear the weight of it."

"So, You think it's heavy?"

"It isn't exactly the lightest of news. Then again, neither was my past with someone like Stoyan Natan."

"Do You..." he paused. Knots tied in his gut. He could not help it. Nor could he release the tension growing at the small of his neck. "Do You think the boys would understand if You told them about all of it and about us?"

"Us?" A voice exclaimed above the snow-covered bushes along the Ku Dziurze stream. "US?!?"

"Tristan?" Andromeda stopped at once, scared more by the fact he heard their conversation than at the information Perseus revealed to her.

"US?!?" Tristan exclaimed again. "You cannot be serious!"

"Tristan..." Perseus began to speak but Tristan raised his hand, demanding he stop speaking.

"Don't." Tristan's temper mixed with disappointment as he shifted his gaze to Andromeda. "How could You?"

"Tristan, we..." she cut her words short, overcome with anguish at the flood of thoughts rushing through her son's mind. She brought her hands to her ears and shut her eyes as they filled with tears. She dropped to her knees, sobbing. "How do I make it stop!"

"What did You do to her?!?" Tristan took a few decisive steps, his hands forming into fists directed at Perseus, ready to defend her.

"I didn't do anything." Perseus spoke slowly, trying to bring Andromeda up from the ground. "She read Your thoughts."

"You're lying!" Tristan hissed back. "She doesn't know how to read minds!"

"She does now." Was all Perseus said. There wasn't anything he could say to make it better - or easier on the young man facing them. He had already made matters worse by revealing to Tristan that Andromeda was able to read his thoughts. It scared the boy to the core. And it made Perseus wonder if Tristan could ever accept him for who he really was.

"Please, stop!" Andromeda pleaded with them both, stumbling to her feet. "Both of You. My head will split into pieces with Your voices mixed in it."

"She really can hear us in her head?" Tristan lowered his hands to the sides.

"Yes." Andromeda wiped her tears away.

"How?" Tristan asked, baffled, scared, and confused.

"It was the poison." Andromeda tried to walk to her son. He took a step back. So, she stopped.

"Did the poison make You drop at his feet, too?" Tristan pointed at Perseus.

"Choose Your words wisely," Perseus warned him.

"Like You chose what to do with my mother?" Tristan hissed out. "You promised me no harm would come her way."

'I caused her no harm. I gave You my word I would bring her home safely...'

Perseus's thoughts, though neutral and sincere in tone, shot like a bolt of lightning through Tristan. He staggered backwards, all but falling.

"What was that?!?" Tristan panicked, scared straight. "What the hell was that?!?"

"It was me." Perseus advised him at half breath, affected as well by what he had done. The effort it took him to channel the words powerfully enough for Tristan to hear them took the wind out of Perseus. And he didn't even know he was capable of making someone hear his thoughts. But now he understood how much it took for Tom to be able to do so.

"Why did You do that?" Tristan swallowed hard, disoriented, and unsure of how he should react.

"I did it so You could see how much I care about Your mother. How much I care about all of You." Perseus spoke with honesty Tristan could not dismiss.

"It's true." Andromeda nodded, holding onto Perseus for balance and comfort. "I would not have fallen for him if I didn't believe he cared about You and Your brothers."

"You fell for him?" Tristan pointed at Perseus. "How is he better than dad? You know what I had to do to save You from him. To save us."

"I know." Perseus spoke up first.

"You told him?!?" Perseus shouted with accusation.

"She did not have to." Perseus shook his head. "Your father fell near where I was standing the day we all met. I heard Your thoughts from where You were standing. I know You pushed him."

"I..." Tristan reached for his heart, then took a step back. So ashamed. So embarrassed by what he did. "You heard my thoughts that day?"

"Yes." Perseus admitted. "I understand why You did it."

"No, You don't!" Tristan cried out. "You don't understand anything!"

"He does." Andromeda inched closer to him. "He really does, more than You think."

"You don't know what I think!" Shouting, Tristan took a step to the side, avoiding her stretched out hand. He turned around and ran behind the cabin. "Stay out of my head!"

"Oh, Perseus." Andromeda broke down in tears as he embraced her. "I hurt him. We hurt him."

"He would have found out." Perseus caressed her face, wiping the tears away. "Sometimes it is better to rip the band aid off in one harsh move. It makes the healing process faster than trying to conceal the truth with lies."

"What is all the commotion?" Alan walked out of the cottage, having a hard time pulling one of the arms through his jacket. "You're back already?"

"Yes." Perseus replied and barely looked at his best friend. Instead, he looked at Andromeda. "I will look for him. Don't worry."

"Please find him!" Andromeda called out after him as he followed Tristan's footprints in the snow, and her worry doubled when Perseus also disappeared into the night.

"Mind telling me what happened?" Alan zipped up his jacket and tried to comfort her.

"I realized I fell in love with Perseus," she sobbed against Alan's shoulder.

"Then that's a good thing."

"It would have been, but I hurt Tristan in the process."

"How could You have possibly done that?" Alan frowned and gestured for them to walk toward the porch.

"He heard us talking about it." She wiped more tears away. They sat on the wooden bench on the porch and Alan tried his best to calm her down.

"Then I am certain he was glad to hear his mother found someone who could keep her safe this time around."

"He wasn't!" She sniffled. "He lashed out at me for it. At us."

"I see." Alan rubbed his knee. "Do You think it would have helped matters if You would have told him about it later? Or would he have reacted the same way if You did?"

"He... would have reacted the same way," she replied, a bit more calmly.

"Then he may have actually saved You both time and effort in the long run," Alan offered her a sincere smile. "Tell me, do You believe Your future includes Perseus in it?"

"That is some direct question." Andromeda tried to smile. She didn't, but the tears stopped flowing.

"Direct, perhaps, but one coming from a place of good intentions."

"You are such a good friend." She sighed. "You are right. I do hope my future - the future of my children - includes Perseus."

"Then You will appreciate Fate for doing most of the job for You just now," Alan nudged at her elbow, which resulted in a faint smile in Andromeda.

"Fate's fickle, isn't it?" Andromeda nudged him back.

"Very much so, my dear. Very much." Alan looked up to search for any kind of sign of Perseus. He found none. "I am sure Perseus will find him."

"I hope so." She wiped away the last signs of tears. "Today was so full of joy. It all turned into despair so quickly."

"Full of joy? Should I suspect today's mind-reading research was a success?"

"Yes. We learned so much about each other."

"Did Perseus tell You more about his parents?" Alan grew quiet for a moment when she nodded. "You know, in a way Tristan's feelings may be similar to the burden Perseus feels deep down because of what happened with his father."

"What do You mean?"

"Did Perseus tell You he blamed himself for their supposed passing?"

"Yes."

"He did? I am glad he shared that with You," he patted her knee. "Did he also tell You how much he cried afterwards? He is and always was a computer tech wizard. Even as a young man no older than Tristan today. He invented a clear, invisible tracking device. But he had a fight with his father, and his parents left for that last mission without the device. Ever since then, the burden of that day never left his aching heart."

"What did You say?" Perseus stood at the corner of the porch, on the other side of the railing. Pale as the snow. With ice-cold sweat rolling down his spine.

166

"Ahh, Perseus. Did You find Tristan?" Alan asked, hesitant, obviously distraught.

"No." Perseus shook his head ever so slowly. "Repeat what You just said."

"About Tristan?" Andromeda chimed in, confused by Perseus's reaction.

"No. About the day I last saw my parents. Where did You hear about the damn tracking device? Where did You hear about the fight with my father?"

"You talked about it." Alan neither moved nor blinked. The only movement that caught Perseus's eye was Alan scratching his knee.

"Never. I only told Andromeda about it today. I have NEVER talked about it before." Perseus's mouth ran dry.

"You must have." Alan's heart paced quickly in his chest.

"Dad?" Perseus whispered in a shaking tone, certain and petrified because the truth was staring right at him...

Chapter 28

Perseus stood there.

Shocked.

Perplexed.

But above all, hurt.

Years. So many years. So many! He had been grieving for the parents he lost. As did his siblings. The Alistairs cried tears of despair and great injustice after finding out their parents, Jade and Richard, perished because of a mission that had gone wrong. They didn't just perish. They were betrayed.

In a wickedly unforeseeable twist of Fate, Perseus and his siblings learned their parents had not, as previously assumed, died. Feelings of grief turned into something neither Alistair was willing to share with the others. Yes, they possessed the ability to read minds, but they honored their agreed-upon golden rule. They didn't cross it. They didn't delve into each other's thoughts when it came to their parents. Not only out of respect toward one another, but also out of trepidation that their own emotions might come to light.

This, if anything, was the one thing Perseus was grateful for as he gazed at Alan, not seeing the man he considered his best friend ever since the day he set foot in the cottage he now called home. The cottage which, just as Alan himself, suddenly seemed foreign and void. Void of peace he longed to feel inside.

As he held his breath, Perseus tried to pretend he didn't hear what Alan told Andromeda. He tried. Was it a wicked twist of Fate? Another in so little time since his brother Rigel met and married the woman whose mother revealed that their parents didn't die after all? Could it have been a coincidence? Could Alan have made it all up? No! A gut-twisting NO! Perseus had never known Alan to make such things up. Alan wasn't wired that way.

Then again, all at once Perseus looked at Alan and didn't recognize him at all. And it had nothing to do with his appearance...

"Dad?" Perseus couldn't decide if that word hurt more by him saying it or by him feeling each letter of it as if three separate jolts of pain were stabbing at his heart from within.

"Dad???" Andromeda whispered slowly, confused more than Perseus at what was happening.

"Perseus..." Alan's mouth ran dry. He always knew a day would come when the truth would be revealed. When he would have to uncover his identity to his son and to his other children. He just did not expect it to happen *that* day because he knew what would soon follow.

"How?" Perseus took a step, then looked at Andromeda and stopped again. "Did You know?"

"What? I don't even understand what is happening?"

Perseus's temper flared. "It doesn't take a genius to put it all together."

"She didn't know." Alan patted her knee, rising from the bench.

"You have been lying to me all these years?" Perseus clenched his jaw. "All this time?"

"I wasn't lying," Alan shook his head.

"Then what the hell would You call it?" Perseus stuck his fisted hands in the pockets of his jacket. Gloves or no gloves, his fists held a grasp so tight he could feel no blood circulating through them.

"I was as honest with You as I possibly could." Alan sighed. If only his son understood the weight of the past. "Under the circumstances."

"Under the circumstances?" Perseus snarled, more hurt than angry. "What circumstances call for lying to Your own son about who You really are?!?"

"It was for everyone's good."

"Whose good? Sure as hell wasn't for mine."

"You would be wrong." Alan began to walk off the porch. Perseus chose not to move. He didn't have it in him to walk up to Alan, and he didn't have it in him to back away. "Your mother and I did what we had to do to protect You. All of You."

"Mother?" Perseus choked up. How foreign that word sounded coming from the man he was facing now. How odd. How inconceivable. "She agreed to it?"

"She was the one who thought of it," Alan explained.

"Yeah, right. What mother thinks of leaving her children behind and intends for them to think she died?" Perseus all but cried the words out.

"One who reads minds. She figured out we were being set up shortly before that last mission," Alan said as calmly as he could.

"What?" Andromeda chimed in. "You knew? And You still went?"

"Yes." Alan inclined his head at Andromeda, taking one cautious step after another in Perseus's direction. "It was the only way to keep You and Your siblings off the Feds' radar. The trail had to end with us."

"What?" Perseus tried his best to control his temper, this time not directing it at Alan. "They found out about us? How?"

"Those few days before the mission after we figured it out seemed so challenging and distorted," Alan stopped a mere foot in front of Perseus. With the moon illuminating his son's eyes, they looked even more piercing.

"How come neither one of us picked up on it?" Perseus cocked his eyebrow, almost mocking Alan.

"Your mother could read minds." Alan replied. "Who do You think taught her how to block someone from reading her thoughts?"

"You?" Perseus asked, trying hard to recall the lessons of mind-reading he had been taught by his parents.

"She could read minds, too? " Andromeda chimed in, overcome with the emotions. "Was she poisoned as well? "

"No. Not exactly." Alan denied it.

"I told her it may be a side effect of being poisoned," Perseus replied with barely enough confidence to sound convincing.

"Huh," Alan nodded. "That is one way of looking at it."

"How did I not recognize You?" Perseus narrowed his eyes on him. "You seem so much older - and don't look the way I remember it?"

"Well..." Alan ran a hand through his gray hair. "Do You remember what You were told about that mission?"

"The no-name contact who met with Tom after the mission told us You and mom died in an explosion somewhere in Europe. No country. No mission details. No leads we could have followed or even start with." Perseus rubbed his eyes. They burned from tears he did not want to shed.

"The man who came to speak with Your brother was the only man at the agency Your mom trusted." Alan looked at Andromeda, then back at Perseus, unsure whether Perseus told her about Rigel or the rest of his siblings. "That man didn't lie, not when it came to the mission. The ambush did result in an explosion, but we studied the land and layout of the compound where we were to meet a double agent we were going to expose. Getting out of there alive was easy. Pretending we passed away and not reaching out to You proved much harder."

"Not from where I'm standing." Perseus whispered in an ice-cold tone.

"I was injured in the explosion. Pretty badly. Part of my face got burned. I underwent multiple surgeries. In a way, that worked out in our favor."

"I'll say." Perseus scoffed.

"We risked our lives to protect Yours. We did so with the determination of parents fighting to keep their children alive." Alan reached for Perseus's arm but he moved to the side. "We discovered a leak of information that was going to affect international relations - and potentially the country's security. The more we uncovered, the closer we got to whoever was pulling strings at the very top. We were going to report it, but then someone figured out we had children."

"Still, You should have told us." Broken hearted, and with a broken spirit, Perseus no longer found it in him to deny the obvious. His father was alive. Alive and standing before him. That mattered above all. Regardless of the pain he felt inside.

"Remember what we fought about that last day before the mission?" Alan reached for his son once more. This time Perseus did not deflect.

"The device failed. I failed."

"It did not fail. It wasn't broken."

"But You refused to take it with You because it would not have worked."

"Not because it would not have worked, but because it would have. And we could not have risked exposing You and Your siblings."

"You let me think it was all my fault? All these years we have known each other?"

"I'm sorry. From the bottom of my heart, but revealing the truth was too risky."

"An apology followed by an excuse devoids sincerity from Your intentions," Perseus said with a hint of a smirk.

"Whoever said those words must have been wiser beyond their years." Alan tried to smile, hoping his son would forgive him.

"Much wiser." Perseus inclined his head, bringing his father in for an embrace that soothed so many broken edges of his heart.

"I'm sorry, son." Alan sobbed as he held onto Perseus.

"You know what comes next, right?" Perseus eased the embrace and saw his father's eyes damp from the tears glistening in the moonlight.

"What?"

"We have to tell the others," Perseus noted, no longer feeling so heavy in the heart...

Chapter 29

As they made their way down to Perseus's underground hidden office, Andromeda was quite impressed by the advanced technology hidden in plain sight. Perseus, on the other hand, tried to decide how to convey the news to his siblings. More importantly, he tried to decide which news to convey first.

Fully aware the timing of the reveal of the information mattered just as much as the delivery, he debated over what to reveal to his family first, and how. Not only that, but he also knew he still had to make Tom aware of Andromeda's abilities. And, in turn, provide sufficient support for her presence during the call.

Was he nervous? That was a no-brainer. After all, he wasn't only dealing with his siblings. He was dealing with siblings who were assassins - and their respective spouses.

In a split second of hesitant decision, Perseus gestured for both Alan and Andromeda to remain out of sight. For the sake of his sister's condition, but essentially for the sake of Alan himself.

"Perseus, to what do we owe this pleasure of speaking at this hour?" Gunay greeted him as the first one to join the call.

"The hour shouldn't be too burdensome for You," Perseus flashed him a quick grin. "The hour is still young in São Paulo."

"Maybe it is, but I'm flying far tonight. I need my sleep to make sure that plane of mine flies effortlessly," Gunay noted, almost patting himself on the back.

"I have never known You to have issues with touching a plane on the ground," Perseus smirked.

"That's because I know to rest before an assignment," Gunay clicked his tongue, winking. "Not like You - two clicks on the keyboard and it's a mission accomplished for You. Sure takes the thrill out of it, if You ask me."

"I didn't ask." Perseus cleared his throat, worried what Andromeda would think of him. "Besides, it's not about fun. You do recall why we signed up for all this, don't You?"

"Maybe for You." Gunay walked over to the high-end sleek glass desk in the office of his penthouse bachelor pad, sat in the white leather designer chair, leaned back, and raised his feet only to drop them - crossed in the most elegant way - on top of the glass desk. "I can't say I don't enjoy the benefits of it."

"I can't say You don't, either." Perseus chuckled, shaking his head. "It's amazing what money does to people."

"It does nothing, Mountain Boy. Nothing. I value the lifestyle I chose for myself. I appreciate what it offers." Gunay pointed at the phone, sat up straight, and pressed a hidden clear button underneath the desktop. The wall behind him, nothing but a single slab of a mirror a moment ago, split in half, gliding the half to the sides into the almost invisible wall pockets. Three monitors lit up. A sleek glass drawer with a top-of-the-line keyboard appeared from a hidden compartment and moved toward him. A couple of clicks on the phone, and Perseus's face flickered on the center monitor.

"You also appreciate the high-tech gizmos this Mountain Boy installed for You," Perseus pointed at himself.

"Can't say I don't." Gunay grinned. He set the phone to the side and stretched out his arms, crossing them behind his head.

"I see You're comfortable." Rigel joined the conversation, greeting his brothers. "What's up, Perseus?"

"I have some news to share with You. But I think it will be best to wait for everyone else," he scratched the back of his head.

"Or we can read Your mind and be on with it." Gunay sighed quite eloquently. "I don't have time to waste."

"You wouldn't dare." Perseus replied in an ice-cold tone, surprising his brothers - and the woman listening to the conversation out of sight. "Besides, the information is too important for me to be repeating myself."

"What's with the tone?" Rigel narrowed his eyes as Jade walked into the kitchen of the dimly lit living room.

"Yeah, man. Is everything alright?" Rasalas wondered, having joined the conversation a moment ago.

"It is," Perseus nodded. "But what I have to say cannot wait."

"Hi, everyone!" Emmeline smiled, with little Atlas cooing in her arms. "Caelum will be here in a minute. He is changing Isla."

"Caelum. On midnight diaper duty!" Gunay laughed. "The world turned on its head."

"What if You're next?" Perseus smirked wickedly.

"Never." Gunay shook his head, amused. "You're next."

"Not before Luna," Perseus answered in perfect timing because another monitor lit up. "Hi there."

"Hi all!" Luna waved her hand, greeting everyone displayed on the laptop monitor as she sat comfortably in her bed in the private quarters at the White House.

"Hey," Rasalas sent her a casual salute, along with the others.

"Ciao," Caelum joined them with Isla in his arms.

"Ciao," said everyone.

"Look at You." Lana mushed over the sight of her brother who couldn't pry his eyes off his newborn child. "Fatherhood sure looks good on You."

"Definitely." Caelum flashed his pearly whites. "But these nighttime feedings take more out of me than assassin assignments."

"And that's why I'm going to stick to what I do best," Gunay saluted him.

"Alright," Perseus spoke as the laughter died down. "We're just missing Tom."

"What is this about, Perseus? You got me worried," Luna advised him, resting her hand on her belly.

"I hope by the end of the call You will feel better," Perseus inclined his head.

"I don't know. You seem awfully cryptic. I don't like cryptic," Lana shook her head.

"I am not cryptic." He stood behind the desk chair, debating whether to sit or stand. No. He could not sit. His nerves would not allow him to sit still when he had so much to say. So much to reveal. So much to share.

"I wonder what's keeping Tom?" Rigel chimed in as he wrapped his arm around Jade's waist. "He isn't usually late for these calls."

"Nor am I late this time," Tom announced his presence in a less than amused tone. "I was out."

"Out?" All those gathered asked in unison.

"You?" Luna sat up in bed.

"Yes," Tom retorted. "Can't a man take a walk down the beach?"

"So, You weren't out." Luna leaned back against the oversized pillows. "You were outside."

"Isn't that the same thing?" Tom moved his shoulders.

"No," Jade smiled sincerely. "Not even to me."

"See?" Rigel grinned at his wife, then directed his gaze at Perseus. "We are all here now. Mind telling us why You sent out the distress signal?"

"Will J.J. join us?" Perseus asked Luna.

"I wish I could tell You. He might, but he's tied up with meetings downstairs," Luna sighed. "If I were You, I wouldn't wait for him to say what You have to say."

"Fine." Perseus scratched the back of his head again, then his bearded cheek. He straightened up and looked at his oldest brother. "First things first. Tom, Andromeda can read minds."

"What?!?" A chorus of voices sounded off in unison. Perseus suspected Tom would lash out at him, but his brother remained silent.

"I spoke with Luna and Gunay about it. I needed to confirm my suspicion." Perseus swallowed hard.

"You guys knew?" Rasalas asked, offended. "What happened to keeping each other in the loop?"

"We... had to be sure," Luna whispered, feeling guilty.

"Well, who better than Tom to figure out if there was another one of us?" Rasalas pointed toward Tom.

'Us...?'

A faint whisper cut through the air. Though Andromeda tried her best not to think as she listened in on the conversation so as not to distract Perseus, she could not help to repeat the word the moment she heard Rasalas say it.

And now, it was too late.

Perseus heard it.

More importantly, his siblings heard it as well.

Whether the grandeur of the situation or the striking reality of it registered in Andromeda's mind.

The room fell silent. Perseus stared at the monitors and saw with undeniable certainty that his siblings staring back at him from the monitors heard what he heard. The whisper of a thought revealing the presence of someone else in the room.

"Perseus?" Tom raised his eyebrows slowly, only to narrow them. "Who's there with You?"

"I am." Alan cleared his throat and took a decisive step forward because he felt Andromeda tense up. He didn't have to be a mind reader to know what it meant.

"Hi Alan," Luna smiled wide.

"Hi." Was all Tom said, in a tone of voice that left no doubt in Perseus's mind he didn't believe Alan was the only one there with him. "Who else is in the room, Perseus?"

"I am..." Andromeda spoke up in a trembling voice.

"And You are?" Gunay inquired, unnecessarily because he already suspected who she was, judging not only by the fact Perseus wouldn't have brought any woman down to his underground office if he didn't trust her, but more importantly by the way his brother took her hand in his as she stepped out of the shadow.

"Andromeda Angelis." Tom said matter-of-factly.

"Yes, that's my name," she whispered, afraid. Perseus mentioned to her that he had siblings she needed to meet, but she had no idea they were so intimidating.

"I wish You would have warned us about this." Tom kept a direct piercing gaze on Perseus.

"There was no time to waste to do this, trust me." Perseus matched his brother's stance.

"Trust You?" Tom crossed his arms at his chest.

'Is she pregnant...?'

Tom's question surprised Perseus, shocked Andromeda, and amused other Alistair siblings - especially Gunay.

"What?!?" Andromeda covered her mouth after exclaiming so loud the echo of the sound boomed along the walls of the underground office. "No!"

"What?" Alan placed a hand on her shoulder.

"He asked if I was pregnant!" Andromeda pointed at Tom.

"She's not." Perseus denied immediately. "This call isn't about her. Not *only* about her."

"Then about who?" Rasalas leaned in closer.

"It's about our father." Perseus paused. Not because he was afraid to reveal the truth, but because he could see Alan was.

"Did You find a lead that could help us search for him?" Luna wondered with hope in her eyes.

"Better. Much better. I found him." Saying so, Perseus turned to Alan, laid a hand on his shoulder, and watched as disbelief painted itself vividly on the faces of those gathered on the other side of the monitors, especially Tom's...

≈ Chapter 30 ≈

"Excuse me?"

Those two life-changing words were the only ones Tom managed to utter. Not that he didn't have much more to say. Oh, he did. But he refused to reveal just how shocked he was to find out that the man they considered to be most genuine was lying to them for years. Or how hurt he felt...

"No way!" Jade exclaimed, relieved beyond words that Rigel would be so fortunate to be reunited with his father - something she wished she would have been able to experience for herself when it came to her own father.

As for Rigel, he wasn't so quick to believe what they had just heard. "Alan? Is this true?"

"I..." Alan's throat locked up. "Yes, it is true."

"And it took You this long to reveal the truth?" Rasalas leaned it closer. He gauged that the storm of emotions rushing through his mind matched that of his siblings.

"I..." Alan paused, suddenly unable to face his children as the man of his true identity, as their father, even though he had spoken with all of them for years.

"He didn't exactly reveal it consciously. He kind of slipped up while speaking with Andromeda, and I put two and two together," Perseus scratched the back of his neck, sending a content gaze Andromeda's way.

"What exactly did You say that lit a lightbulb in Perseus's brain?" Gunay asked Alan with narrowed eyes. "It must have been profound if he finally figured it out."

"Hey!" Perseus protested.

"What?" Gunay retorted, pointing to Alan. "You've been friends for years and not once did You notice anything familiar about him?"

"Shut up." Perseus hissed out, offended. "You all got to know him. Don't blame this one on me."

"No." Alan spoke up, searching for strength. "Blame me for it. It was my burden to carry, my decision to bear."

"Why?" Rigel asked, aware that Luna kept silent, as did Tom. However, Luna did so with tears in her eyes.

"To keep You safe," Alan whispered. "All of You."

"You don't look like the man who came to visit my grandfather?" Emmeline wondered, full of doubt because she never noticed any similarities she could have possibly noticed in the year since she met Alan. "You look so much older."

"You are right, my dear," Alan nodded. "I had a minor procedure done before we came to see Your grandfather. We had to ensure I could walk the streets without causing too much of a stir. Scars - especially those across the face - don't usually go unnoticed."

"And then?" Caelum inquired, reading his wife's mind, and agreeing with her.

"And then I paid for Your mother's safe passage across the ocean, and for Richard's surgeries." Emmeline's grandfather startled everyone as he announced his presence, which almost resulted in Caelum swearing aloud. He leaned in between his granddaughter and his grandson-in-law to get a better view of his longtime friend. "Hi, Richard."

"Hi," Alan waived.

"It's good to finally be able to call You that," Emmeline's grandfather smiled wide.

"Let me get this straight," Caelum turned to him. "You knew who Alan was all this time, yet You said nothing?"

"*Veramente*," agreed the grandfather. "That's correct."

"Why?" Emmeline turned toward him.

"Because *he* said nothing," the grandfather pointed at Alan.

"You..." Luna choked up, hugging her belly. "You're really alive?"

"Who's alive?" J.J. walked in, immediately alarmed at his wife's facial expression and her tensed up body posture.

"He is," Luna whispered, finally allowing her tears to flow freely now that she leaned on J.J. as he sat beside her on the bed.

"Oh, hi Alan." J.J. waived at the monitor. "Why wouldn't he be alive? Did I miss something major?"

"He's my dad. Our dad!" Luna sobbed, hugging J.J.'s arm.

"Richard?" J.J. leaned away to see her better, then turned to look at the man looking back at him with a remorseful gaze.

"HE'S MONROE???" Andromeda switched her stare from the monitor to Perseus, then back to the monitor.

"Hi there." J.J. sent her a casual salute. "You must be Andromeda?"

She nodded, speechless that the President of the United States of America himself was aware of her existence.

"Double damn, then. Pleased to meet You," J.J. grinned from ear to ear.

"That... explains a lot," Andromeda blinked, barely acknowledging anyone else joining on the call.

"What does it explain?" J.J.'s grin disappeared.

"Perseus referred to You as his dear friend," she noted, hoping to find the courage to speak with the President in a tone of voice that would not reveal just how affected she was by speaking with him.

"He did?" J.J. grinned once more. "Double damn."

"It also explains why he quotes You so much," Andromeda added before she could stop herself.

"He does?" J.J. raised his eyebrow, amused. "When did he quote me?"

"That's not the point of this call, Monroe." Perseus puffed out air, embarrassed. "The point is that we found our father."

"We?" Rasalas asked, skeptically.

"We," Perseus hugged Andromeda.

"Tom, will You say something?" Alan spoke slowly, cognizant of his eldest son's silence. It never spelled out anything positive. Ever. That, he knew all too well.

"Where's mom?" Tom said so dryly and matter-of-factly it hurt Alan deep down.

"She is... in hiding," Alan replied with caution.

"Where?" Tom continued.

"I cannot reveal that information," Alan stood his ground.

"Alright. *Why* is she in hiding?" Tom crossed his arms.

"First of all, one cannot walk around in plain sight after being pronounced as deceased," Alan noted. "Second of all, we realized the second bottom Feds figured out Your mother possessed the ability to read minds. Then they figured out we had a family. We did everything in our power so that they wouldn't be able to trace You all."

"What???" Tom breathed as a cold sweat rolled down his back.

"The man who came to tell You of our passing was the only man we could trust. We took a risk by asking him to speak with You, but it was the only way." Alan sighed heavily. There was so much he wanted to say. So much he wanted to reveal. But this wasn't the time. This wasn't the occasion. "My friend was certain we passed away. We needed him to believe it, because we needed You to believe it."

"So, You chose to lie to us all this time?" Luna asked in a shaking voice. "So many years. I cried for so many years."

"I am sorry, my sweet Moonbeam, but it was the only way," Alan offered her a smile, though tears had dampened his eyes.

"An apology followed by an excuse devoids sincerity from Your intentions," Tom clenched his jaw.

"Oh, shut up Vega!" Luna scolded her oldest brother, sobbing even more. "He called me Moonbeam! How can I be mad at him?"

"Pregnancy hormones?" Gunay looked at Luna.

"Yup," J.J. embraced his wife with tenderness.

"I can't help it!" Luna chuckled, wiping tears away. "Putting Tom's brooding aside, I hope You can stay on the call for a while. We have so much catching up to do."

"Thank You, my dear," Alan inclined his head. "But I think we have to start with something more important."

"What could be more important than revealing You are their father?" Andromeda inquired, surprised.

"Well, I would say that a proper introduction of You to everyone is more important at the moment," Alan winked at her with a fatherly gleam in his eyes. "Everyone, You know who Andromeda is. Would You please let her know who You are?"

"Oh." Andromeda's cheeks turned ruby red. "Hi everyone."

"We'll go first," Luna smiled sincerely. "My name is Luna, and this is J.J., my husband."

"Mr. President." Andromeda almost curtsied, to which Jade giggled because Andromeda's reaction matched that of the one she had not so long ago when President J.J. Monroe led her onto a dance floor the day they met.

"It's J.J.," he clicked his tongue. "I hope You don't mind if we ask You to keep this little encounter private. All of it."

"I understand," she agreed. "From what Perseus told me, having an assassin for a brother-in-law isn't the safest of information for a President of the Free World."

"Perseus told You we're all assassins?" Luna smirked. "Well, some of us used to be."

"Yes." Andromeda inclined her head, sending a comforting look Perseus's way. "You can rest assured I will keep that information to myself."

"And they all read minds," Jade chimed in, earning an almost undetectable smirk from Rigel.

"Were You all poisoned?" Andromeda was shocked.

"What?" Rasalas raised his eyebrows, confused.

"I... led her into believing her sudden ability of reading people's thoughts was a result of the poison," Perseus swallowed hard, feeling guilty because Andromeda tensed up in his arms.

"Led me to believe?" She turned to him.

"You mentioned it. I just ran with it. It seemed to be a better explanation at the time than revealing the truth," he replied, feeling sheepish.

"And the truth was???" She raised her chin, not in protest but rather out of concern.

"He used a vial of my blood to save You. You were on the verge of not surviving." Luna explained, ensuring she looked directly at Tom while saying so since he was the one to have made the decision to administer the live-saving vial.

"But how is that related to me suddenly hearing all these voices in my head?" Andromeda shook her head with disbelief.

"Luna's blood gave You her ability to read minds," Rasalas hissed out with resentment Luna understood all too well.

"How is that possible?" Andromeda gazed from Perseus to Alan.

"Their mother was born with the gift of reading minds. They inherited it from her," Alan tipped his head. Seeing Tom's thunderous gaze, he chose not to say anything more. "She also had a certain gift of healing faster than others. Luna was the only one to have inherited it."

"Will it go away?" Andromeda wondered.

"Hasn't for us," Rasalas brooded even more profoundly.

"Don't worry. It won't harm You. But it might get a bit annoying - especially with this Alistair brood," Luna beamed at her. "Anyway, I am the youngest of all of us. And Tom - Vega is his real name - is the oldest."

Rigel smiled and decided to speak to avert the attention away from Tom. He didn't dare to read his brother's mind, but he was certain if he had, nothing positive would come out of it. "Rasalas, Caelum and I are triplets. And this is my wife, Jade."

"You share the same name as Perseus's mother? It must be so nice," Andromeda smiled from her heart.

"That's a long story." Jade reciprocated her smile.

"And Perseus and I are twins - though I won't deny I'm definitely the better looking one," Gunay sent her a smug smile.

"Speak for Yourself." Caelum chuckled wickedly, pointing at himself. "Best-looking genes swim in these veins."

"Easy, Fin Boy." Emmeline scolded him as she passed to him the child she held in her arms. "Don't mind him. You would think fatherhood humbled him, but no. My name is Emmeline, and that's Atlas and Isla. We also have a daughter, Anya, but she is asleep."

"Very pleased to meet You," Andromeda waved a hand. A feeling of gratitude filled her heart to see such a close-knit family. Something she always hoped for in all the years she felt all alone in the world. And because she had not learned or even been made aware of the possibility of blocking her own thoughts, the Alistairs heard her thoughts. Especially Rasalas, who rose to his feet, unable to sit still.

"Do You have any kids?" Emmeline asked, even though she already knew. Nonetheless, she tried to make Andromeda feel welcomed because of the way she had met the Alistairs herself.

"I do," Andromeda brightened up. "Tristan is 15 years old, Liam 11, and Kai is 9."

"And You all managed to fit inside Perseus's mini log cabin?" Gunay smirked.

"Yes." Perseus brooded, staring directly at Gunay.

"Alright." Gunay raised his hands in a sign of surrender. He decided to switch gears and posed the question on everyone's mind. He leaned in and looked at his father. "So, do we still call You Alan? Or Richard? Or dad...?"

Chapter 31

There were so many things Perseus had regretted in life. Not saying goodbye to his father all those years ago when neither of them knew it would turn out to be Richard and Jade Alistair's last mission. Not apologizing to his father for his outburst of anger at himself because of a device he assumed had failed. Not being able to admit to his father that he looked up to him as much as he did...

Losing his parents broke him. Losing his father broke him. But finding out that Richard Alistair had become his best friend in disguise was even more earth shattering. Not because Perseus ever considered himself a gullible man. On the contrary. He considered himself to be honest and loyal. Especially, when it came to family.

Alistairs were as close to one another as siblings possibly could. And yet, after learning their parents' Fate they chose to disappear from everyday life and moved away from their home. Too afraid of what would happen next, too scared to face the reality of a parentless life together. They were strong, but an event like that proved just too overbearing.

They made a vow, though, that doomed night they all gathered in their secluded homestead's living room for the last time. They would go undercover. Each under a covert name, an assumed made-up profile, with a factitious past backed by data developed by Perseus himself. They would infiltrate all layers of the invisible powers responsible for Richard and Jade's betrayal. They would explore all possibilities, leave no stone unturned until they would find out the truth about what really happened and who stood behind the disloyalty that changed their lives forever.

Alas, they kept coming up against one dead end after a dead end. Until Richard Alistair himself confessed he lived right under Perseus's nose all along...

"I must tell You, facing all my children and their families as the man I really am was harder than I thought..." Richard sighed heavily as Perseus closed and locked the door to his office behind them once they made their way up when the hours-long call finally ended.

"It would not have been so gut-wrenching if You told us the truth from the beginning." Perseus patted him on the back.

"Ouch," Richard winced.

"You should be more careful," Andromeda scolded Perseus, and let out a yawn she was unable to stop.

"It's alright, my dear. The pat didn't hurt, the wisdom behind Perseus's words did," Richard grinned.

"They can say what they want. They can brood all they want. They will come around. I would give anything to see my father again..." Andromeda embraced Richard with care.

"You cannot begin to imagine how being able to finally reveal the truth felt. How much seeing the love in Luna's eyes felt." Richard embraced her back. "Being able to share that moment with You made it all the more special."

"Well, it made it scary for me." Andromeda shivered. "I had no idea finding out about the assassin thing was so insignificant compared to everything else."

"Really?" Perseus smiled, amused.

"Yes." Andromeda admitted. "Who knew an assassin could be friends with a President?"

"Or that a President could be worthy of being our brother-in-law?" Perseus smirked, pointing at himself. "Believe me, Monroe didn't have it easy with us. President or no, we had to make sure he was worthy of our baby sister."

"President? Worthy?" She laughed.

"You bet." He turned to Richard. "Monroe didn't have it easy. Imagine how much harder he would have had to try if we knew You were alive?"

"Fate doesn't quite work that way, son. Luna may not have ever met him if You knew I was alive. Rigel may not have fallen in love the way he did if he knew Your mother was alive. So much happened since the last time my dear Jade and I saw each other for the last time."

"Don't You miss her?" Andromeda looked up at him as they made their way toward the kitchen table by the window.

"With every beating moment of my poor old heart," Richard laid a hand over his chest. "We parted ways with the faith that our sacrifice would not have been in vain."

"Why not just tell us where she is? Caelum can read Emmeline's grandfather's mind and find out where she went into hiding," Perseus crossed his arms at his chest.

"You would not dare." Richard warned him, yet his gaze warmed up after a moment. "There are laws that govern life and universe You cannot work against. All actions lead to consequences. If forced, some decisions end up hurting You in the long run. The easiest way usually isn't the best one."

"But if You follow the flow, it may end up leading You to what's meant for You," Andromeda sent Perseus a loving look that struck him right in the heart.

"Exactly, my dear." Richard agreed. "My dearest Jade understood all too well that the only way to ensure Your survival was to allow those who plotted against us to celebrate our demise."

"Doesn't it bother You in the least that those bastards walk free while we have to hide?" Perseus set the kettle. He needed something hot and strong to calm his nerves. And coffee was the only option he would settle for.

"It does. That, it does." Richard sighed heavily and sat across Andromeda. "But we have to believe righteousness wins in the end. Your mother always believed it should. That's why I fell in love with her."

"Why didn't You go with her, wherever she's hiding?" Andromeda set her chin on a folded hand, yawning.

"We had to part ways to ensure both of us wouldn't get caught. She left Europe. I needed the surgeries to reconstruct my face. The only man who could provide the level of confidentiality lived here in Poland. He was a veteran of the Polish Underground Army. This was his cabin."

"You never mentioned it before?" Perseus frowned. "Why did You tell me this was Your place?"

"Because it was." Richard shrugged his shoulders. "My friend died before I rescued You that day. But he taught me a lot about these mountains."

"Is that why You know so much about the hidden underground tunnels and passages?" Perseus leaned back against the kitchen counter.

"Yes. The Polish Underground Army used them during World War II, but they existed for centuries." Saying so, Richard turned to Andromeda. "Do You know where The Eye of the Sea got its name?"

"I heard a legend years ago that there is an underground passage linking the lake with the Baltic Sea?" Andromeda grinned.

"That would be accurate," Richard tipped his head while Perseus smiled wide. "But it's more than a legend. It is a fact. There are passages linking the mountains with the Mediterranean Sea, too."

"There aren't." She chuckled, shaking her head.

"Wouldn't be so sure." Perseus clicked his tongue.

"Perseus is right." Richard pointed at his son. "He knows his way around the mountains and passages. I may have shown him a few entrances to the caves and tunnels, but once he caught wind of the underground network, he took it upon himself to explore every nook and cranny hiding inside the mountains."

"I gladly accepted the challenge," Perseus clicked his tongue again.

"A man with an aching heart found solace in the loneliness the mountains offered," Richard nodded with conviction. "But I hope he found something more."

"Did he?" Andromeda gleamed at Perseus.

"I hope he did." Perseus smiled at her.

"Is Tristan back?" Kai interrupted the conversation, startling them.

"What?" Andromeda rose from her chair. "Did he not return yet?"

"No?" Kai rubbed his eyes. "He's not in the room."

"He's somewhere out there?!?" Andromeda rushed to the door, reaching for her jacket frantically. "It's all my fault!"

"No, it isn't," Richard tried to calm her down as Perseus reached for his jacket.

"Stay with the boys. We will find him," Perseus nodded at Richard. "If we are not back by sunrise reach out to Tom. He can help us find him."

"Alright." Richard crossed to Kai to comfort him, when suddenly Perseus's Tatra Volunteer Search and Rescue emergency phone rang loudly.

"Damn it." Perseus swore. He picked it up. And swore again in his thoughts - forgetting Andromeda could read his mind.

"What is it?" She asked in a shaking voice.

"Thanks for letting me know. Don't worry, I'll stay inside," he ended the call, and pointed at Richard. "DO NOT leave the house. There were a couple of avalanches near the Gorge. Ana told me not to go into the mountains until later in the day when they can figure out the severity of the damage."

"Tristan!" Andromeda covered her mouth. "We have to find him!"

"You have to stay with Richard and the boys." Perseus turned to his father. "Go downstairs. Call Tom. There's no time to waste."

"Go! Go now!" Andromeda took Kai's hand and watched with worry as Perseus disappeared into the night...

Chapter 32

Perseus considered searching for people atop the Tatra Mountains range to be his second nature. He knew the mountains inside out. Literally. The peaks, the valleys, the gorges, the tunnels hidden beneath the snowy ground only few were aware of. He saw saving people as the yang to his yin. A much-needed balance without which he could not function. He believed in the righteousness of each rescue as a form of so-called repayment for each life he took as an assassin.

And yet...

Searching for Tristan got to him on a level he never experienced before. Tristan wasn't some lost nameless tourist. He wasn't someone Perseus held no connection to. That young man was so much more to him. More with every passing day.

True, Perseus felt guilty about the way Tristan found out about his relationship with Andromeda. He felt remorseful about terrifying the young man by revealing he possessed the gift of reading mind. Though - Perseus admitted wholeheartedly - if it weren't for the way Tristan had reacted to the news of their relationship, Perseus never would have attempted the ever so exhausting act of connecting with Tristan's mind to whisper to him that he was a good man who would never ever hurt Andromeda.

He felt... stricken with the deafening fear magnified by a fatherly concern for their child.

Was he Tristan's father? No, of course not. But he knew blood granted by Fate ran thicker when compared with water. Or with a bloodline.

And the longer he searched for Andromeda's son, the more he understood and valued his connection with Alan. Or whatever Alan meant to him as a father figure.

"Tristan!" Perseus's raspy throat kept locking up in the nightly mountain breeze after nearly two hours of calling out his name. To no avail.

'What's taking You so long?!? You had no problem connecting with Emmeline...'

Perseus's thought traveled seamlessly to Tom's mind. Although not without a hint of a spiteful insult.

'Offend me. Go ahead. See if it will bother me as much as it will bother You when I decide to stop helping You...'

Tom retorted stoically without giving Perseus's attitude any consideration. He sat restlessly in his worn-out black leather chair in the rustically furnished living room of his residence located inside one of the seaside caves of Cathedral Cove in New Zealand and concentrated all his efforts on trying to locate Tristan.

'We should have picked up on his trail by now...'

Perseus grit his teeth out of worry mixed with anger.

'I share Your sentiment. I do. But when it came to Emmeline, she was the one who sought a connection with me when Caelum was shot, remember...?'

Tom exhaled, upset with himself for not finding any trace of Tristan's thoughts - although he refused to share that frustration with his brother.

'Yeah, well, You may have had it easy with Emmeline, but what about Jade...?'

Perseus inquired, swearing aloud as he slipped while trying to make his way up the mountain.

'What about Jade...?'

Tom crossed his arms at his chest, well aware of what Perseus had in mind.

'You connected with her across oceans...'

Perseus stopped at once. Not to listen to Tom's thoughts, but as a precaution. Though it was still dark, Perseus knew the mountains like the back of his hand. He knew the land's layout, the way the trees around him moved to the gentle pre-dawn breeze, the way the ground lay still - undisturbed in the dead of the night. He also knew the barely detectable silent sound nature made shortly before a coming avalanche. So, he stopped and listened. With eyes closed and heart opened to the surroundings.

'I got him...!'

Tom shouted, aloud and in his thoughts.

'You do?!? Where is he...?!?'

Perseus opened his eyes at once, turning left and right to look for him as if the young boy was mere feet away from him.

'He can wait! You have to take cover! That avalanche You anticipated in Your thoughts is coming down. Tristan saw it, it barely missed him! But You have got to run to the nearest tunnel...!'

The urgency in Tom's voice scared Perseus more than his warning. He turned back, and ran to the closest tunnel entrance, swearing aloud as he slipped and fell on his knee as the avalanche fell right behind his back, blocking the tunnel's entrance.

'Damn it! Double damn it...!'

The blocked entrance wasn't the problem. The sharp pain splitting his knee was. He tried to stand. And fell again.

'Are You alright? Perseus, are You alright?!?'

Tom shouted with concern. He could barely pick up the trace of Perseus's thoughts before the snow rolled down the mountain. Now his worry multiplied tenfold. He rose from the chair, unable to sit still, and paced back and forth in the small living room scarcely lit by dozens of antique lamps.

'Yeah, I'm alive. All good. But my knee doesn't share the sentiment...'

Perseus crawled, limping, to the nearest cave wall and used it to stand up. His knee hurt unbearably. But he had to go on. He had to move. He had to find Tristan.

'When You find that lad, thank him. If it weren't for him, You wouldn't have made it...'

Tom smirked, relieved Perseus was safe.

'First I'll yell at him for running away. Then I'll thank him...'

Perseus grit his teeth and began to move deeper inside the tunnel.

'Do both, but first we must find him again. I think I figured out where he was when I heard him thinking about the snow coming down the mountain. But I need to be sure...'

Tom rolled up the sleeves of his sleek black shirt. He decided the best way to connect with Tristan would be to do so outside, barefoot, with waves of the gentle surf amplifying his connection. He walked out of the caves and directed his steps toward the nearby shoreline. He removed his shoes and walked into the surf up to his waist.

'Please tell me You can find him. There aren't that many lost tourists along these mountains...'

Perseus's pleas grew louder and more worrisome.

'Give me a moment, will You? I may have a shot at this if You stop screaming inside my head about Your bruised knee...'

Tom hissed out impatiently. He closed his eyes, spreading his arms out, then dropped them to the side, allowing the strong waves to flow through his fingers.

'And...?'

Perseus clenched his fists from pain. Tom remained silent. Thunderously silent. Uncomfortably silent.

'He's... he's...'

Tom mumbled to himself, picking up on Tristan's thoughts, and debated whether he should tell Perseus that the young man's thoughts revolved around Perseus. Solely around him.

'Well? Damn it, Tom. I'm at a crossroads in this tunnel. I need to know which way to turn...'

He realized he should not have raised his voice at Tom, but he couldn't help it. He had been up needly 24 hours by now, his knee shot jolts of sharpest pain he had ever felt, and above all he needed to find Tristan and bring him home safely.

Home...

The moment Perseus thought of it, the ache he felt in the knee disappeared for a second. It was replaced by a pang right in his heart. Home. That word no longer held the same meaning it did a little over a month ago. His home changed. His life changed. He changed. Not just because of the woman he saved. But because of the three boys who in some odd sense saved him. Saved him from a life of loneliness he thought he chose for his own benefit.

'Perseus! Perseus! Can You hear me...?'

Tom's concerned voice brought Perseus back to reality.

'Yes. Sorry. I thought I got lost...'

Perseus rubbed his knee, and somehow the pain no longer bothered him as much as it did before.

'Well, who wouldn't? But don't worry. I found Tristan...'

Tom opened his eyes with a piercing gaze.

'Is he safe...?'

Perseus asked. Finding Tristan was no longer a problem. His safety was.

'Yes. You won't believe where he is...'

Tom placed his arms at his hips, realizing how cool the waters around him had turned.

'Where...?'

Perseus grew exasperated. He was facing entrances to five tunnels leading to different mountains. He needed to be certain he chose the right one.

'He's at the cliff where he pushed Stoyan. And he's not in the best shape, emotionally...'

Tom explained slowly, choosing to keep Tristan's thoughts to himself. It wouldn't do any good to share them, especially with Perseus...

Chapter 33

Perseus stood at the entrance of the cave atop the cliff where so many lives changed not long ago. He stood there, watching as Tristan sat on the snowy ground, with his back against the mountain slope. Sat and shed silent tears because he was too upset to hold everything inside, yet too proud to cry aloud. And Perseus understood his emotions. All too well...

Was Tristan's father like Richard Alistair? No, not by a mile. But Perseus knew that both fathers' professions weighed heavily on their children's paths in life.

Did Perseus and Tristan both carry regrets when it came to dealing with their fathers? Yes, and he comprehended with absolute certainty that Tristan would forever bear the burden of choosing to sacrifice his own father to save Andromeda - even if she wasn't his real mother. Especially, since she wasn't his real mother.

So, Perseus stood there, in silence, and contemplated how to best approach Tristan without terrifying him. And the best option that came to his mind was to announce his presence from where he stood. From afar. Hoping to high heavens Tristan wouldn't run because his injured knee would not cooperate if he had to chase him.

"Don't be alarmed." Perseus's calm voice, as steady as he could have afforded, broke the silence of the dawn, with the sun rising shyly above the mountains.

"You?" Tristan raised his bowed head, distraught, but did not move.

"Please, don't run. I just want to talk." Though it hurt to even stand, Perseus gathered all the strength he had, demanding of himself not to swear with each step he took, and made his way to where the young man sat.

"What the hell happened to You?" Tristan turned his head away, quickly wiping his tears hoping Perseus would have seen any trace of them, and tried his best not to reveal he did care about Perseus's condition.

"I decided to partake in a little race with an avalanche. Sadly, I lost." Perseus clenched his jaw and sat beside Tristan, grunting from pain.

"A man like You shows pain?" Tristan mocked him.

"A man like You dares to call upon hell? Didn't Your mother raise You better than that?" Perseus replied, noticing it surprised Tristan he referred to him as a man.

"She's not my mother." Tristan retorted with resentment.

"She is, the way she cares about You" Perseus inclined his head, looking toward the horizon.

"She doesn't."

"Ah, but she does." Perseus breathed heavily. "Some people are better at parenting than others."

"You have no right talking about my family. Sleeping with her doesn't give You that right," Tristan fisted his hands.

"That's a bit uncalled for." Perseus tensed up. Then he recalled the way the Alistair brothers - him including - grilled J.J. Monroe after finding out he was involved with Luna. Was this how it felt on the other side? Was this how it felt to be on the outside? Was this how it felt to be determined to want to be included? Yes, it was. Realizing so, Perseus nodded to himself. "It may be a direct deduction, but still, it is a bit uncalled for, don't You think?"

"No." Tristan shook his head, covering it with his hands. "We never should have hidden in that stupid shed of Yours."

"But You did. And it saved Your lives. It certainly saved Andromeda's." Perseus looked at him, then at his injured knee, examining it. "You should take full credit for it."

"Should I then take credit for the way my father died, too?"

"Hey." Perseus nudged Tristan. "Don't do that."

"Do what?"

"Don't blame Yourself for what happened to Your dad."

"You don't know how I feel..." Tristan began to rise. Perseus stopped him by holding onto his arm.

"Don't leave. Please."

"Why? Because You can't run?" Tristan took his gaze off Perseus and looked at the way he was holding his arm.

"No" Perseus let go of Tristan's arm. "Because You and I have more in common than You think."

"What on earth could we have in common - aside from caring about Andromeda?"

"So, You admit I care about her?"

"You better. You wouldn't dare leading her on if You didn't," Tristan sat back. "She had too much of that with my father."

"I am sure he loved her at least in some way," Perseus noted, but Tristan shook his head.

"He loved himself more than anything else - or anyone else. She made him look good, and served his purpose for a while, but he didn't love her."

"Sometimes parents are hard to understand," Perseus sighed. "But life has an odd way of showing us the meaning of their parenting."

"More like the lack of it." Tristan scoffed, running a hand through his hair. "It took me a long time to accept her. Then when I did, I realized how much she decided to suffer through for my safety."

"And for Your love," Perseus pointed out. "You know You matter to her. Believe it or not, You matter to me as well. You and Your brothers do."

"Why should I believe You?" Tristan turned to him. There was so much resentment in his eyes. And just as much sorrow.

"Because I am being honest with You. You are not a child. Your life may not have been easy because of Your father's actions, or his parenting, but it caused You to see the world for what it is. That is as much a burden as it is a gift."

"Yeah, well, I didn't ask for such a gift or burden," Tristan looked back toward the horizon.

"And I didn't ask for a gift of reading minds." Perseus puffed out air, then held his breath because he tried to adjust his position but all it did was aggravate the injured knee.

"Can You really read people's thoughts?" Tristan asked with suspicion.

"Yes." Perseus nodded, then chuckled, looking down. "Little good did it do, though. My own father, presumed dead for years, has been living right under my nose."

"What?" Tristan's neck all but suffered whiplash. The shock in his voice amused Perseus.

"So much has happened since You ran off," Perseus patted Tristan's shoulder. "I guess I owe You big time for doing that."

"Me? You owe me for running off?" Tristan tipped his head back, confused.

"Yes, because You ran off, Alan tried to calm Andromeda down, but inadvertently revealed he was my father."

"Alan is Your father?" Tristan leaned forward, even more confused. "Why did You say he was presumed dead?"

"Because he was. It's a long story," Perseus grinned, glad to have peaked Tristan's interest.

"It doesn't look like we're leaving anytime soon with that bruised knee," he pointed at Perseus's leg. "How come You didn't recognize Your own father?"

"Because he worked for the government, discovered information about double agents, had to stage his own death to save our lives, had reconstructive surgeries because he was injured in the process, and ended up befriending me in an odd twist of Fate."

"He befriended You and didn't say who he was?"

"Nope."

"Why?" Tristan moved a bit closer.

"Because by that time my siblings and I became government-paid assassins to try to find out the truth about my parents' passing."

"So, the brothers You mentioned are assassins?" The color washed out of Tristan's face.

"Yes. Oh, and my sister is married to the President of the United States."

"What?!?"

"I wouldn't shout while we're up here. Avalanches are nasty buggers if You ask me, especially if Your voice calls them out."

"Does the President know Your sister is an assassin?" Tristan leaned in, whispering, as if he did so out of fear of being heard and not because of the threat of a possible avalanche.

"Yes, he does." Perseus's smile widened. "But she doesn't do that anymore."

"Did her assassin's membership expire?"

"You are definitely Andromeda's son," Perseus chuckled and patted Tristan's back. "She said the same thing."

"She knows?"

"Yes," Perseus admitted. "I knew the time would come for me to be honest with You. This is as good a time as it will ever come. I want to be a part of Your family."

"What?" Tristan sat back, shocked.

"I want a future with Andromeda. And that future needs to include You - all three of You." Perseus grew quiet for a moment. Somehow saying those words to Tristan, high up on the cliff where Tristan thought their life almost came crashing down irreversibly made those words even more profound. Perseus didn't read his mind, though. He didn't have to. He saw what he needed to see in Tristan's eyes.

"Have You... asked my mother about it?"

"So, now she's Your mother again?"

"I always felt that she was." Tristan looked down. "Please don't tell her what I said about her earlier."

"Don't worry. Your secret is safe with me," he nudged Tristan. "And I hope You will keep the information about my family a secret as well."

"Of course," Tristan promised. "I am well aware families keep shadows hidden from the public eye."

"That, they do." Perseus chuckled but grew serious. "I am not a picture-perfect man, Tristan. Nor will becoming a part of my family be safe. But I give my word to You, here in witness by the rising sun and these mountains, that I will guard You, Liam, Kai, and Andromeda with my heart, body, and soul."

"If that isn't worth everything, I don't know what I would define as family." Saying so, Tristan embraced Perseus in a hug they would remember for the rest of their lives.

"Double damn..." Perseus whispered with tears Alan would most certainly describe as a father's right. "Let's get out of here. If we don't come home soon, Your mother might get lost in the mountain tunnels looking for us."

"There are tunnels in these mountains?" Tristan wondered with curiosity as he helped Perseus to his feet, taking a hefty amount of Perseus's weight on his shoulders when they turned toward the cave entrance from which Perseus emerged.

"You bet." Perseus clicked his tongue, grateful for his newfound son's help. "I might as well tell You about everything else You should know since I'd like for You all to live with me."

"Everything? How much more is there?"

"Well, how about I start by telling You about the search for my mother, who also went into hiding to keep us safe?" Perseus whispered, indebted to his mother and father for allowing Fate to guide their lives the way it had done thus far...

≈ Epilogue ≈

If someone asked Perseus Alistair for the meaning of love not so long ago, he not only would have dismissed the question, but he also would have laughed it off. Love was a burden. Love was some antiquated notion only few believed in. Love was... an oddly peculiar feeling that had somehow befallen his siblings.

And, yet...

The man he was now, he accepted love with all his heart because it got to him, too.

He was an assassin. He was a loner. He was a self-centered Mountain Man macho with a misplaced hero syndrome who realized that the love he tried so hard to evade finally caught up to him. In every way possible. And he vowed to never take it for granted. Why? Because in a whirlwind of Fate's fickle he became a father to three amazing sons who made him understand what being a father really meant.

And he hoped to high heavens the woman who was the boys' mother would love him as much as he loved her.

"You do remember I can read minds, too. Don't You?" Rising on her elbow, Andromeda smiled at Perseus as they laid in the oversized sleeping bag atop the Tatras Tower in the Štrbské Pleso region of Vysoké Tatry, Slovakia. The view from the Tower was breathtaking. The fact they watched the moonlit sky bathed in millions of stars in the dead of the Snow Moon night made it all the more meaningful.

"I do." Perseus smirked, attempting to mask his sudden bout of bashfulness because he was caught off guard. "I meant everything You read in my thoughts."

"That You hope I love You as much as You love me?"

"Yes." He reached for her hand. "I also meant the part about becoming a father to Tristan, Liam, and Kai."

"There's that misplaced hero syndrome."

"Wicked woman." He chuckled and pulled at a strand of her hair. "You keep bringing that up, I'll make my family call You Milksop. Especially Monroe."

"Fine. Your misplaced hero syndrome stays between us."

"Then, so shall Milksop."

"Agreed." She nodded and looked up at the sky. "Isn't it amazing our troubled paths crossed the way they did, when they did?"

"I wouldn't call it amazing."

"What would You call it then?"

"I would call it worth the heartache." He ran his finger along the contour of her chin. "To think I almost lost You before even knowing how much Your love would heal me."

"Heal You?"

"I was a lonely man. I thought I liked being lonely."

"That kind of went out the window with me and the boys taking up every nook of that cabin," she chuckled.

"And I would not have it any other way. Ever." He exhaled, aware she would have been able to hear his thoughts.

"Do You mean it?"

"About You reading my thoughts? Of course."

"Not just about that," she tipped her head. "Though, I have to admit reading others' minds is not as scary as knowing Your siblings can read minds as well."

"Why? We cannot help being born the way we were."

"That is not what I meant. Reading minds is one thing. Knowing someone close to me can read my thoughts scares the Milksop out of me."

"You think of my family as being close to You?"

"Yes," she agreed. Wholeheartedly. "And I do hope Your family will come to think of me that way, too."

"Even Monroe?"

"I cannot believe he's Your brother-in-law," she paused for a moment. "Do You think Tom will warm up to me one day?"

"Of course, he will. He warmed up to Jade and Emmeline, and even to Monroe."

"Maybe You are right. But I feel like he does not trust me."

"It is not about You. It's about Your ability to read minds."

"Why?"

"We are not Your usual white-picket-fence kind of family. We are far from it. Trust is vital to ensuring our safety - and survival. Not everyone respects that enough to keep it a secret."

"I do."

"I know that. Tom knows that, too. Even if he shows otherwise." Perseus shifted, and sat up, allowing the gentle sway of the safety net atop the Tatras Tower to dictate the way he sat, facing Andromeda. "We trusted someone long ago. She was the first person we trusted after learning our parents lost their lives. Let's just say sometimes things can go from bad to worse."

"I'm sorry," she touched his bearded cheek. "Tom can rest assured I won't break that trust. I have been hurt too much in life to realize when I found home. A true home. That kind of feeling should never be taken for granted."

"It won't, on my part." He grew serious, linking their hands together. "I love You."

"Perseus..." she choked up. "I love You, too."

"Damn. It felt easier to talk about this with Tristan."

"You talked with Tristan about Your feelings?"

"Yes. When I found him after the avalanche. And earlier today," he cleared his throat, visibly nervous.

"You did?"

"Yes. Actually, I spoke with Tristan, Liam, and Kai."

"You did?" She repeated.

"Yes. I find talking with the boys quite refreshing - and very rewarding because they have so much to say."

"And they don't bore You?"

"Never. Especially after finding out that my Christmas gifts to them were more of a hit than a miss," he smiled. "Who knew Tristan liked carving in wood and Liam was a fan of astrology?"

"Don't get me started. Did You see the way his eyes shone with tears of joy at the telescope You gave him?"

"To be honest, the box of wood carving tools and the telescope belonged to me for years. I didn't have much time to prepare the gifts," he rubbed his beard. "Kai was the hardest to shop for, if You ask me."

"Well, for a man who hadn't spent much time with kids, I'd say Your gift to Kai was extraordinary. He has never been to the sea. That blue amber orb made his day. He told me on more than one occasion that the gold specs inside the orb shine brighter than the sun whenever he holds it up to the light."

"Yeah." Perseus grinned. "It was a present from Gunay from one of his assignments in Dominican Republic. I caught Kai holding it up to the kitchen window in the morning."

"See?" She brought her hand to hold his cheek.

"I like Your smile. That gentle subdued smile. The one that makes me wonder what's hiding behind that smile. That's my favorite."

"You know what's hiding behind it. You can read my mind. You'll always know what I'm thinking. You Alistair men are probably the only ones who will know what women have in mind during an argument."

"What if I told You... I can teach You how to block someone from reading Your thoughts?"

"Now You tell me?!?" She exclaimed, and the mountain air echoed her voice far into the distance. "Why didn't You teach me before?"

"Because in order to learn how to block others' thoughts, You first need to accept reading them without showing everyone that You can." He leaned closer. "Reading minds isn't just some fun trait made for parties. It's a responsibility not many can handle. You have to figure out a way not to be affected by others' thoughts. To carry Yourself in front of a person whose thoughts speak to You, without that person knowing it."

'I didn't think of that...'

"Not many do," he leaned forward. "Going into hiding all those years ago wasn't such a burden to me. We had to learn to live with the ability to read minds in a way that would not reveal the truth to others. Not everyone welcomes You with open arms once they figure out You can see right through their little lies. My siblings found their way of dealing with it. I found mine. And living alone was a kind of a blessing."

"I bet it felt heartwarming when Alan... sorry, Richard accepted You and Your talent the day You met."

"It did." Perseus scoffed. "I bet I scared the living daylights out of him the day he saved me in the mountains. How do You look Your own son in the eye after doing everything You could to make sure he thought You were dead?"

"He did explain why he did it, though."

"He did," Perseus agreed. "Let me tell You, becoming a father figure to Your sons made me realize how profound of an impact my father's decisions made on his - and our lives."

"A father figure?" She repeated after him. They had so little time to think of their future. Of what they hoped it would take them. Of what they hoped to accomplish. Of what they hoped to bring to each other's lives.

"Yeah," he murmured. "I also talked to Richard about us."

"Us?"

"Yes." How come it was so difficult to speak of his feelings? He realized why. Because he never had to explain them to anyone before. And now that he needed to do so, he felt almost ashamed and scared to admit them.

'Perseus Alistair, didn't I mention a moment ago I can read Your mind...?'

Her gaze moved him as much as the directness of her tone.

"Andromeda Angelis, I cannot spend another moment not knowing if You would agree to be my wife."

"What would it change?"

"Everything."

"Everything? Can't You come up with enough words to at least make up a whole sentence?"

"It would change everything. Knowing I would belong to someone - to You."

He didn't finish the sentence. Her blank stare gave him no warning, no clue as to her intentions. Her lips, pressed at once to his, rocked him. All of him. Even the part that somehow felt damaged because of the years of forsaken loneliness. "Should I assume You share my feelings?"

"Oh, shut up!" She kissed him again. "You really can't take a hint, can You?"

"What hint?"

"For a man who reads minds, how is it possible You didn't figure out I fell in love with You the split second of a heartbeat I opened my eyes and saw You for the first time, staring at me with those deep angry eyes of Yours?"

"That first day?" He opened his eyes wide. "I thought You couldn't stand me?"

"I guess You should be excused for that. After all, You hadn't had much experience with women," she winked mischievously, only to giggle as he tickled her side.

"You're no Milksop. No respectable Milksop would insult an assassin the way You just did," he laughed lightly.

"Listen, Alistair," she pointed at him. "I may be a novice at this whole mind-reading thing, but we're equal now. Be good to Your soon-to-be wife or I might take up assassindom and show You who is better at it."

"Double damn!" He spread his arms out and high toward the sky in a sign of the most gratifying feeling he had ever felt. "I'm the luckiest man alive!"

"Shhh!" She reached for his arms, bringing them down. "See if You feel the same way come springtime."

"I will." Perseus cupped her face. "Heavens above and all our lucky stars will attest to that."

"Do You mean it?"

"You have my word." He kissed her so tenderly she smiled, sighing against his lips, but he paused abruptly. "My garden grows Blue Hollyhocks. I like the way their scent fills the cabin in summertime."

"Who knew a Mountain Man macho could be such a romantic?"

'Perseus, You've got to get back home...'

Gunay's urgent voice rang loud and clear in both Perseus and Andromeda's thoughts.

'What is it...?!?'

Andromeda replied before Perseus could.

'Right... I forgot You can hear me as well...'

Gunay thought, surprised at her sharp and quick response.

'What is it, Gunay...?'

Perseus repeated Andromeda's question.

'I think we finally found our first clue to finding mom...'

Though cautious about it, Gunay was certain of what he and Caelum uncovered. Dead certain.

'You did...?'

Perseus replied with a rush of excitement rather than resentment rushing through his blood.

'Yes. We think we picked up on her trail...'

Gunay paused, blown away at what he was about to reveal.

'Well??? Where is she...?'

Perseus asked with the urgency of a son desperately awaiting most favorable yet feared information that would soon change all their lives.

'She's here... near São Paulo...'

Gunay swallowed hard as a promise of a new adventure washed over him.

'You know what that means, right...?'

Perseus smiled slowly, nodding to his beloved Andromeda.

'Double damn, I do! I'll show all of You how professionals deal with these kind of affairs...'

And show them all, he would. But not before his heart would show him first...

≈ TO BE CONTINUED ≈

Thank You for taking the time to read the story that inspired my imagination and allowed me to pen the story on paper.

If You enjoyed it as much as I have enjoyed writing it, please feel welcomed to leave a review on the book's Amazon page.

Sincerely,
J.M. KÆ

Please feel free to visit my Author Website for more information about other published books.

www.joannakurczakwriting.com

- Coming soon -

SPITEFUL CHARADES

BOOK IV OF THE ALISTAIR SAGA

J.M. KÆ

≈ **Chapter 1** ≈

São Paulo. Rich in culture. Full of architectural wonders. Steeped in centuries-old traditions. City, which Gunay Alistair found to be the perfect cover for his life. His undercover life. Life of a nameless, always elusive, assassin living up to the reputation of the greatest con artist in history. And he firmly believed himself to be one without the slightest shred of a doubt.

Did he love being an assassin? Of course. Was he forced by Fate to choose this path of life and no other? Yes. But he always knew deep down he would have become one inevitably. Why? Because he loved it. The intrigue. The secrets. The secret missions. The thrill of it all.

Did he pity his targets? To some extent. Yet he reckoned it worked in everyone's favor because he only accepted assignments targeting the worst criminals, the worst offenders, the worst of the worst.

But he had a vice...

That vice was his family. His parents. His siblings. His past.

His parents were the main reason he became an assassin. His siblings were the reason he chose to move as far away from them as possible. His past was the reason he worked alone. Not because he ever failed at his job - he NEVER did. But because he failed as a man years ago. And his heart never forgave him for it...

"It really is such a pity to waste an entire trip on one business meeting." Gunay murmured as if to himself while pretending to savor the taste of stale champagne, dressed in a perfectly tailored high-end tuxedo. He was leaning against the column on a second-floor balcony with a crystal champagne flute in his hand. The rather mediocre bubbly did nothing for his taste buds, but it played its part as a prop. He held it up to his lips whenever he wanted to hide a disdained smirk. He turned it in his hand to appear interested in the atmosphere around him. He ran a finger up and down the length of the flute as a sign of allure to the few women he found worth his attention to pass the time. Bored, he looked across the grand ballroom and spotted the most ignored and most dolled-up woman in the venue.

'Show time...'

He thought, making his suave way down the marble staircase of Villa Milanese on the tropical island of Galapagos.

To those around him, he played it stoic and cool while flirting with the overly enthusiastic floozy whose only ambition in life was to collect millionaires, one way or another. In reality, though, Gunay scanned the room for the reason he attended the carouse. His next target.

"Yeah. I pity You," Roberto Sivrice, Gunay's security tech and best friend, whispered in the earpiece device with sarcasm.

"You should..."

Gunay's unimpressed tone amused Roberto. He knew perfectly well how much Gunay loathed cheap champagne, and loathed cheap millionaires even more. "A couple more hours, and You'll be relaxing down at the beach with Rasalas."

"Sounds amazing." Gunay smirked, unintentionally siding with something the flirtatious floozy said. Her long red hair, slicked back into an immobile braid, did nothing to accentuate her natural beauty. Neither did the white designer gown. Yet both were overshadowed by the dazzling jewelry she was practically drowning in.

"I know, handsome." The woman linked her hand through Gunay's arm and leaned in closer. "I knew the moment I saw You that You were the type of a man who knew how to appreciate the effort it takes to look this unforgettable."

"You would be correct." Gunay sent the woman a well-trained half grin. Women loved the gesture. He loved the effect it had on them.

"Is she really that unforgettable?" Roberto chuckled in Gunay's earpiece.

"*Veramente*," Gunay whispered, masking the wicked cockyness of his tone with a sip of the bubbly, and leaned toward the woman to make her think he was speaking to her. "Any man who fails to admit Your beauty to himself is but a fool unworthy of Your presence."

"Oh, stop it." The woman brushed a hand down his chest, obviously taken with his charm.

"Yeah. Stop it," Roberto cackled in a mocking sound.

"I am very fortunate to have accepted the prospect of a business venture with our host tonight," Gunay continued with his usual one-liners. "To think I would have lost out on the chance to meet You if my assistant would have declined the invitation."

"It would have been such a shame." She ran her fingers up the lapel of his tuxedo, unbothered by the idea of being so obvious in her intentions. After all, no one bothered to look their way. The crowd of self-absorbed millionaires was too busy with their own business. At least that's what she thought.

"Yeah, such a shame." Roberto clicked his tongue, clearing his throat afterwards.

"Maybe You and I can venture onto the beach after my business meeting concludes?" Gunay slowly skimmed over the woman's face, lingering his gaze on her lips. "My yacht is anchored not far from the shore."

"You certainly know how to make a woman wonder," she smiled.

"That makes two of us." Roberto raised his eyebrow, impressed by his best friend's effortless talent of captivating women. "Just remember to handle the business meeting You came there to handle. And that You flew and not swam there."

"Definitely, darling..." Gunay whispered, answering to both.

"Darling?" Roberto shook his head. "I've been called worse."

"Definitely." Gunay raised the champagne glass to his lips, running a finger down his momentary companion's neck. And froze.

There she was...

Damn the whole world, planets, and universes!

There... she... was...

The one...

The only one that got away...

Alarmed by Gunay's held breath and galloping pulse, Roberto sat up in his chair and double checked his best friend's vitals transmitted via

Gunay's watch. A spike so sudden and so disconcerting was never a sign of anything good. In fact, it spelled out trouble. Ominous and formidable trouble.

"Gunay? Gunay?" Roberto rose to his feet. "What's wrong?"

"She's here..." was all Gunay was able to whisper, almost inaudibly.

"She...?" Roberto tipped his head back, confused, then opened his eyes wide. "No way!"

"Way..." Gunay swallowed hard, unable to move, unable to blink. He swore at himself on the inside. He was looking at the woman he once loved, if only for a heartbeat. A heartbreaking heartbeat too long. Iuliana Selenio...

Made in the USA
Columbia, SC
09 February 2025